One WESTERN Town

PART 2
A NOVELLA

DAVID QUELL

WESTBOW
PRESS
A DIVISION OF THOMAS NELSON

WestBow Press books may be ordered through booksellers or by contacting:

WestBow Press
A Division of Thomas Nelson
1663 Liberty Drive
Bloomington, IN 47403
www.westbowpress.com
1-(866) 928-1240

ISBN: 978-1-4497-6593-4 (sc)
ISBN: 978-1-4497-6592-7 (e)

Library of Congress Control Number: 2012915937

Printed in the United States of America

WestBow Press rev. date: 09/17/2012

To my Father in heaven
To my father who's soul is in heaven
And to my mother for her love and compassion

CHAPTER 1

'Blessed is the man who walks not in the counsel of the wicked, nor stands in the way of sinners. Nor does he sit in the seat of scoffers. But his delight is in the law of the Lord. And on this law, he meditates day and night. He is like a tree.'[1]

Jacob Quaid was that tree. Quaid stood tall yet was grounded firmly in faith. He had a muscular build.His broad shoulders were supported by a thin waist. Those rounded mounds filled his shirt all the way to the summit. It seemed as if they could carry the weight of the world, and they often did. From there, Quaid's long arms extended out like branches from the trunk. His biceps were well defined. They were hidden, however, by a blue, double-buttoned shirt. Quaid had worn it so often, it had now grayed. Quaid's hair was a dirty blonde, a mix of sun and sand. Thin and fine, it was not in any way wavy. It was cut tight and cropped at the ear. Smart and sophisticated,

---

1   Holy Bible - Psalms 1

it suited the young lawman. His hair blew easily in the breeze yet fell back to its original station. Quaid covered his hair with a hat. Tall and ten gallon, it rested majestically above his brow. The hat was a part of Quaid, as much as his eyes, teeth, and mouth. It belonged there just as much as Quaid belonged in the law. Weathered and wearied, the white of the hat was all but gone. On Quaid, though, it worked. The hat matched the kerchief around his neck. It hung, this small and corporeal cloth, dangling and decorative. Its golden fibers were woven full and unwavering. Even in the mightiest of winds, the fabric appeared to be cast firm, as was Quaid's determination.

As with his clothing, Quaid had aged, and more than his twenty-plus years reflected. The formation of his facial features were solid. A stone rock jaw appeared to support the promontory peak nose, all the way down to the firmament base of the chin. Sparkling in the midst of this mountainous man were green glowing eyes. Like foliage in the sun on a summer's day, they shone. The wrinkled lines above the brow dug in like trenches, giving Quaid an earthly appearance. The dirt dusted his dermis from his forehead to his neck. The only refuge from the oxidative elements eroding Quaid's countenance was the rounded brim of that broad hat.

Down from the waist jutted sinewed legs, as if they might take root. Quaid's quadriceps were large and strong. Their formidable fibers filled his beige britches as if he were an elephant. Around his waist was a holster. It was leather with an oversized brass buckle. This gave Quaid's standard attire a little flair. Quaid's gun was off the hip. The firearm was hardly noticeable on his massive frame. By now, the weapon had become a part of him.

Quaid's feet were big, but covered by shoes, not boots. The shoes were leather and had low tops with laces. They were soft and flexible like an Indian's moccasin. To Quaid, the fit was so good he never really noticed the confinement of the tarsals and metatarsals.

Quaid's hands seemed to tell the story of his life's struggles. Parched, dry, and cracked, they had seen much work. The skin was tanned, almost leathery to the touch. Quaid's palm was square and wide. Each finger broad, stemmed out like a post. Yet the cuticle was clean and neat, the trait of a gentleman.

Quaid was the son of a Union soldier and a socialite mother. He was eloquent and polite. His exquisite manner, friendly smile, and gentle demeanor reflected his mother's early efforts. Because of her caring, Quaid grew to be a man of respect, dignity, intellect, and conscience. He was fully aware of the immense consideration that was to be given to all life. His mother was responsible for mining these traits. She loved him as God had loved him. For God so loved the world that he gave his only begotten son. Though often demure, Quaid had a voracity for fairness,even as a child. His character had a fired determination to excel.

As a small boy, a young Quaid challenged his oversized father to wrestling matches on a regular basis. In each instance, young Quaid approached his formidable father, unafraid. This day, with his dad down on his knees, young Quaid attacked first. The small grappler, grunted and grimaced,wrestling with the large ursiform man. Young Quaid leapt to the animal's back, digging his fingers deep into its hide. The animal wailed loudly. It swung its paws around with a savage fierceness. Young Quaid dug deeper. The beast stood, spun, and wiped Quaid clean from the rear, like removing so much dust from one's clothes. The young boy flew across the room, landing firmly on the floor. The jarring thud rattled the wrestler. The throbbing pain pulsed through his muscles. Unabated by the anguish, young Quaid rose and faced his opponent. He burst into full stride, and hurled himself like a projectile. Again the brute swept his imposing posture across the oncoming attacker, sending the boy careening back. Banged and bloodied, the boy crawled up to his feet. Without hesitation, young Quaid approached. Looking for an opening, the boy wound around his prey and then, sprang. Thrusting his form forward, young Quaid struck the biped in the hindquarters. Shifting his weight, the boy pulled and arched backward in an attempt to bring this mammoth to the floor. It was to no avail. Struck down once more, young Quaid gathered himself. His mind raced. The boy's thoughts were scrambled and crazed. Fury filled him. Blinded by madness, he struck out. With all his will, young Quaid swung wildly at the ferocious figure. The blows landed on target over and over. Tears of frustration and pain poured out and over young Quaid's cheeks. His father decided to end this contest once and for all. The elder encircled young Quaid with his massive appendages, and held tight. The boy was wrapped up in coils of contracting, concrete, fibers. Unable to move, and barely able to breathe, the boy relinquished as more tears flowed. Once his father felt the boy's body go limp, he leaned in close to his ear.

"I love you," he said softly, "please stop."

Young Quaid, hearing these words, came back to his body and regained control. Young Quaid, still weeping, could not speak. His father, realizing this, kissed his wet cheek and said,

"You are my son, ... my boy."

Slowly, his father released his grip, setting the boy free. Again his father addressed him.

"Jacob, you are passionate, but you must learn a directed discipline."

The boy smiled and said, "I am sorry, I love you too, father."

At this early age, through his father's teachings, Quaid became an accomplished horseman, dogged tracker, and patient patriarch.

Quaid, later spent a large portion of his formative years being reared by his uncle, Robert. This was subsequent to the tragic loss of his father in a barn fire, and his mother to consumption. Quaid relived the combustive accident that claimed his father's life each night in his young mind. The nightmarish episodes seemed to slow the movement of events as a wound-down watch tells time. Every second ticked agonizingly, as young Quaid witnessed the carnage. The bright white flames flashed up into the darkness. He could feel the heat drying his eyes, even before he was able to shed a single tear. The ever-expanding energy held him at bay. This, as the pyrolytic blaze burned a hole deep into his soul. Desperate, young Quaid called out with such a force as to shake the angels.

"Father!" he would cry.

His Herculean exertion created no resonance. Motionless and mute, young Quaid ignited from inside out. Dropping to his knees, he hung his head. The helpless boy sat, staring at his world, enveloped in hell's fury. After the calamity, young Quaid's mother contracted consumption. To the young boy, it did seem that his mother was consumed; not by her disease, but by the pernicious void left by the loss of his father.

It was then that Quaid travelled east to live with his uncle. Robert Quaid, being a man of the cloth, immersed young Quaid in God's teachings. Young Quaid thrived in the Word. In study, obedience, and prayer, young Quaid developed a full heart. That heart was in the law of God. For young Quaid loved the Lord, and the Lord loves justice. Young Quaid worked diligently to preserve those laws in the name of justice.

Quaid recalled one of his earliest conversations with his uncle. It fell on a certain Sunday morning in May. The sun was shining brightly, as if to light the way to knowledge. As he walked to church that day, young Quaid could hear the birds of the air. Each sweet sound resounded. To Quaid, it was as if he were bathing in the gentle music of the notes. The atmosphere was crisp and clean. Young Quaid took full each breath, and soaked his lungs with oxygen. Peace was upon him, God's peace. It was the day of the Lord, the day young Quaid devoted to Him.

Upon arrival, young Quaid went inside the chapel, staying close to Robert. The stained glass reflected the colors of the rainbow across the pews. They had arrived early and were temporarily alone. Young Quaid took a seat, then, kneeled. Robert opened his Bible and looked down at his nephew.

"I think this passage sounds appropriate," said Robert.

Robert began to read,

"'The Lord bless thee, and keep thee. The Lord make his face shine upon thee, and be gracious unto thee. The Lord lift up his countenance upon thee, and give thee peace.'"[2]

Young Quaid was serene. It was as if all his troubles had been lifted, and washed away. Young Quaid looked up, and he smiled at his uncle; comfortable in his new home.

Robert Quaid was a gentle soul. His demeanor was cool. He harbored, however, a firey faith underneath. Headstrong and caring, relentless and loving, determined and understanding, firm and forgiving; these were the qualities found in Robert Quaid. Robert's forthright delivery of the English language reflected his broad based erudition in art, music, literature, and philosophy. As a priest, he was very communicative. Robert was generally happy with his station and vocation. As a father figure, these traits flowed over into young Quaid's early life and development.

After prayers were completed, Robert turned to young Quaid to talk.

"Jacob," said Robert.

"Always remember, God is just. So it must be in you. For, he is in you."

These three short phrases were the cornerstone which was to build a life. It was a life which aspired to service; service to the law, service to the Lord.

To young Quaid, his uncle's porch was a place of solitude. He often would go out and sit on the wooden bench to contemplate his world. Inside were the trappings of an old farm house. It was dark with few windows. Cold and drafty it was, even on a hot summer

---

2   Holy Bible - Numbers 6:24

day. The floor and walls were solid oak. As one walked across the floor; each step created a crescendo of crackles. The front room was a combination of a main room with fireplace, and a dining area with a large block table. The surrounding furniture was indistinct. Wooden chairs, a rocker, and a bench filled in the space. A large colorless rug garnished the floor. The kitchen was in the back of the house and it had a separate entrance. The windows were adorned with drapes of brown and tan. They fell flat, leaving the opening exposed, even when the shutters were closed. The kitchen also had a hinged door that could raise up from the floor, and lead to the cellar. Young Quaid's aunt would store jars of food in this cool, damp, dungeon, to help preserve the nourishment for a future date. Two small bedrooms spun off each side of the kitchen. The rooms were modest. They held just a bed, a bench, and a chest of drawers for clothing. Young Quaid's aunt and uncle had a tall armoire with which to hang his aunt's particulars. It was the one piece of extravagance in the entire house.

Beyond the back entrance of the kitchen was a stunted well. It was stone. Drinking water and laundering were found here. Beyond that was the barn. Made of old wood, it stood strong against the fields. It had no color; all had been washed away by weather. The barn held two horses, two goats, four cows, and some chickens. It also was the home of young Quaid's best friend, Poe.

Poe was a grey wolf that had been found abandoned in the wilderness by his father. Wolves ran in packs. When one was injured, or deemed inferior, the wolf cub was cast out. Poe was one such defective. Young Quaid's father was resolute in his belief that the strong should care for the weak. To that end, young Quaid remembered the day his father brought him home. He had cradled that little bundle of fur in just one hand. The young cub's eyes were deep, saddened, and robin egg blue. The fur was soft as goose down. It was not feathery though, more of a prickly textured smooth. Young Quaid nuzzled this furry form against his chubby white cheeks. Surely heaven had many rooms full of furry friends such as this. Young Quaid immediately fell in love. This lost soul would be saved. Young Quaid would raise him as his own. And he did. Young Quaid and Poe spent hours playing in the tall grass of the fields. Through this love, young Quaid saw that the wolf club showed the character trait of a great protector.

The naming of the cub was a story in itself. Young Quaid's mother being of good social standing; loved following the singers, writers, and philosophers, of the day. One perorator of the pen had caught her attention. He was different. He was dark. He was decadent. Damning were the words he wrote. His sonnets, however, whispered the longings of love lost, so powerfully. Even the mountains moved at the mention of his megrims. She drew young Quaid into this eclectic world of wonder. Young Quaid read the words most ferrevently. When it came time to name his new found friend, young Quaid recalled the tragedy, the pain of loss, and the endured sufferings of loneliness of his companion. Only one name came to mind, Poe.

Living outside the city, young Quaid enjoyed growing up on a farm filled with animals, open sky, and vegetation. Life was simple but not easy. Chores kept young Quaid occupied most of the day. When the work had been completed, he would spend time talking to his uncle.

"Could you tell me about my father?" young Quaid asked.

"Not much to tell," said Robert. He continued.

"You are already aware, Jacob, that he fought for the Union in the war between the states."

"Yes," said young Quaid.

"He was a brave man. Quite skilled," said Robert.

"What do you mean, skilled?" asked young Quaid.

"I think that story is best left for another time," responded Robert.

After a short pause, young Quaid continued, "I want to learn to fight."

"Fighting is one matter. Protection is another," said Robert.

"But I suppose Poe will not be around forever," said Robert looking down at the beast lying at the young boys feet.

"I will teach you to defend yourself, Jacob."

Robert Quaid began a campaign to familarize the young boy with an assortment of weaponry. Yet, this did not occur in the fashion that the young boy would expect.

One gorgeous spring morning, as the sun bathed the foliage in yellow and white, Robert gave a command to the boy.

"Jacob, go out to the side of the barn and I will join you presently," Robert said.

Young Quaid, eager to hold and fire a weapon, ran as fast as his legs could carry him. Visions ran through his head of holding that silver, sleek, six-shooter. The joy of pulling the trigger; the explosive power he would possess; the satisfaction of seeing the projectile finding its mark; all indelible wonderment he thought. When young Quaid reached the grass next to the barn, he turned and looked toward the house. He could see his uncle carrying something over his shoulder. It appeared long, and wooden. A rifle, young Quaid thought. What a delight it would be to become acquainted with this injurious instrument. As his uncle drew near, young Quaid was not quite sure what he was carrying. Now, only ten feet away, Robert slung the instrument from his shoulder to his waist. Young Quaid could clearly see it was an axe.

"See all that wood behind you?" called Robert.

Young Quaid turned and saw a large pile of uncut trees.

"I want you to go to the chopping block over there," Robert pointing as he spoke, "and cut all that timber into small pieces."

Visably upset, young Quaid retorted, "I thought you were going to show me how to use a weapon." There was a pause, young Quaid continued, "You know, shoot a gun."

Robert could tell by the forelorn expression on young Quaid's face that he was disappointed.

"I said I would teach you to defend yourself," said Robert. "The defense of one's being comes in many forms, Jacob. The avenue I have chosen for you may not be what you expect but trust in me to deliver on my promise."

Young Quaid was dejected but willing. What other choice was there, he thought. Young Quaid walked over to his uncle and took the axe from him.

"Wait a minute," cried Robert. "I want you to hold it like you are going to shake hands." Robert took back the axe, and held it out for young Quaid to try again. Young Quaid stretched out his right hand and grasped the handle.

"Firm," said Robert, "but not too tight." Young Quaid followed the instructions.

"Good," said Robert. "We can begin."

That afternoon, young Quaid chopped block after block, after block, of wood. He piled up the pieces high; then, even higher. At the middle of the day, Robert came out from the main house.

"Here is some cold water. Please drink, Jacob."

Young Quaid swallowed it down in a couple of gulps. It was right from the well. It was cold, clean, crisp, and quite refreshing. A small amount of the liquid escaped from the cup and spilled over onto young Quaid's shirt. It felt good. Young Quaid sat down in the shade of the barn. Robert strode over and sat next to him.

"A good morning's work," Robert said.

"Work is right," young Quaid mumbled.

Robert smiled then placed his arm around him.

"Jacob," he said, "anything in life worth having will take work. That includes the skills it takes to defend yourself."

Young Quaid glanced up at his uncle.

"I am not sure I understand," he said.

"You will my son, you will," replied Robert.

Robert stood up and turned to walk back to the house. He hesitated. Then he turned back towards young Quaid.

"Jacob, you are done chopping wood for today."

Young Quaid grinned from ear to ear; he dropped the axe, and ran for the house. Robert shouted,

"Wait one minute!"

Young Quaid froze. He knew that meant something else was coming. Robert shouted.

"You are done chopping wood, but I want you to carry that axe with you for the rest of the afternoon."

Young Quaid looked at his uncle perplexed.

"What?" Young Quaid asked.

"I want you to take that axe with you wherever you go. No matter what you do the rest of the day, you must have it in your possession. That means you cannot set it down, or let it go, for one second or one minute of the day," said Robert.

Robert continued in a firm yet understanding tone.

"If you want to learn, Jacob, you will do as I ask. Have faith my good son. Have the strength to trust in that faith; and you will be rewarded."

"I do not know if I can," said young Quaid.

Robert approached young Quaid and stopped. Robert, then, as he so often did, quoted the Bible for young Quaid.

"'But also if ye shall say unto this mountain, be thou removed, and be thou cast into the sea; it shall be done.'"[3]

Young Quaid took Christ's words to heart. He carried the axe everywhere. He never set it down once. At the end of the day, at the dinner hour, young Quaid was anxious to tell his uncle of his accomplishment. Young Quaid pulled his chair close to the table, so that he could easily converse with his uncle. Eager to talk, young Quaid started even before his uncle could sit down.

"I did as you asked," said young Quaid, brandishing the axe hanging on the back of his chair.

---

[3]   Holy Bible - Matthew 21:21

David Quell

"I carried it all day. All of the time."

Robert raised his head up, reached over, and patted his nephew on the head.

"Good work," he said.

"Now repeat that feat five more times."

Young Quaid looked up in shock. His mind raced.

"What are you saying?" young Quaid asked.

Robert smiled.

"It was a good day's work, Jacob. That is of no doubt. However, to complete your task you must repeat today's heroics five more times."

Young Quaid was still. Stunned, he could not speak. Robert realized the disbelief that had filled the young man like the cold water from the well. In an effort to encourage the boy, Robert again quoted the Bible.

"'And on the seventh day God ended his work. And he rested on the seventh day from all his work which he had made.'"[4]

Robert paused.

"You see, Jacob, even God worked tirelessly to complete his work before resting. Should anything less be asked of you?"

Embarrassed, young Quaid replied,

"No, I suppose not."

Young Quaid was as good as his word. He carried the heavy- laden axe wherever he went. He smiled through the awkwardness. His fatigued arms pained through every long hour. At last, the six days had come and gone. Young Quaid awoke early with the sun. Suprisingly, young Quaid discovered that his uncle was already outside standing next

---

4   Holy Bible - Genesis 2:2

to the old barn. Robert started speaking as young Quaid approached.

"Now that you have become accustomed to this weapon, I will instruct you on its use."

Young Quaid looked at his uncle perplexed. He questioned,

"What about learning to use firearms?" After a pause, young Quaid said "I want to learn to shoot."

"All in good time," said Robert. He turned, bent down and grabbed some wet mud from the ground. Robert smeared an X on the side of the barn.

"Here," Robert said. "I want you to hit this X, every time without fail."

Young Quaid responded, "With what?"

"Why with that axe you are holding," said Robert.

Young Quaid could not believe his own ears. Robert walked over to him and took the axe from his hand.

"Hold it like you are going to shake hands," Robert demonstrated. He continued,

"Then draw it back, and let it go."

End over end the axe traveled through the air, cutting through the daylight like water flowing downstream. Thud! It struck the barn hard and embedded itself deep in the wood, right at the center of the X. Young Quaid grinned.

"Can I try?" he asked.

"Certainly," said Robert. "Let me tell you one last thing before you begin."

Again there was a slight hesitation as Robert contemplated how to deliver this monumental phase.

"This was your father's weapon of choice." Robert continued. "He was an expert at close range combat. The battle axe, knives, and often his bare hands were all that he needed."

"Needed for what?" asked young Quaid.

"That story is best left for another time," said Robert.

A determined young Quaid practiced day in and day out. He became adept at the axe. He then moved on to knives.

"This is a belt knife," said Robert, pulling the small sharp-edged instrument from a burlap sack. Holding the short, thin, cutter up to the sun, it sparkled. The blade was half the length of the knife. The handle was wooden with a small piece of metal separating it vertically from the blade. The blade of the dagger was not wide, but had a pointed tip. Robert continued,

"These were carried tucked into a soldier's waistband. A larger version may be held in a sheath. These knives were multifunctional.

"Multifunctional?" asked young Quaid.

"They could kill," said Robert.

He then reached down into the sack and took out another.

"This is a Dirk," Robert said.

The blade was much longer, and thin like a nail or spike. The end of the handle was nickel. From the thin tapered point, the blade extended double-edged, unlike the belt knife.

"This beauty is German crafted. The Southern version was often called an Arkansas toothpick."

Robert reached down again, extracting yet another.

"Now this one here is a clip-point."

Pulling the large blade from the sack, young Quaid watched as it seemed its length extended forever. It was over 17 inches long, with a staghorn handle. Looking closer at the Bowie blade, young Quaid could read the words, 'The Patriots Self Defender.'

"This clip-point Bowie is British in origin. Very useful."

Useful for what? young Quaid thought.

"You will learn to master each blade," said Robert.

Young Quaid became familiar with the old Bowie. He worked hard hitting that X with every attempt, using every weapon.

After many a day, Robert came to check on his student. Robert watched with glee as young Quaid impaled the barn time after time with accuracy.

"Now you are ready to fire a gun," said Robert. "We start tomorrow."

The following day, Robert again had beaten young Quaid out to the barn. Young Quaid ran as fast as his legs could carry him to the spot. Robert had one leg perched on a box, the other on the ground. Robert knelt down on one knee. He opened the box and pulled out a large wood and metal hand gun. It was so big, young Quaid thought it would take two hands to hold it.

"This is a Colt Dragoon," said Robert.

"Why is it so big?" asked young Quaid.

"Jacob," said Robert, "you will become proficient with this cumbersome model first. In that way, when you start using the latest designs, it will be effortless."

Young Quaid understood. When he looked down at the Dragoon, he saw its vast length. How could he even get it in and out of the holster, young Quaid thought. Robert handed young Quaid the massive mauler. He tried to grasp it with one hand and almost dropped it.

"Load it, like this," Robert instructed.

Young Quaid raised the heavy piece, aimed and fired at the barn. Boom! Off went the firearm. Young Quaid's arm jerked back a little; and the projectile crashed into the side of the barn.

"Try again," said Robert.

Young Quaid again raised and fixed the Dragoon. Boom! Off it went again with similar results, missing his intended target. Young Quaid felt dejected. His shoulders slumped down. His countenance became sullen. Robert walked over to him and placed his hand on the boy.

"Try this one," he said. Robert pulled out a Navy. "It is a little lighter and more accurate."

Young Quaid again repeated the sequence of firing. He did this over and over. Young Quaid started to see improvement. Robert stood quietly by and allowed young Quaid to work through his difficulties. After exhausting his ammunition, young Quaid stopped. All was still. Young Quaid turned toward Robert.

"Continue," he said, Then he walked back toward the house.

Hours turned to days. Days turned to months. Later, Robert approached young Quaid slowly.

"You see Jacob, it does come to you with time and practice. There is no substitute for hard work." With that, Robert held out a Colt revolver, double action.

"This is the state of the art," he said.

Robert proceeded to describe all the working parts in great detail. His knowledge was surpassed only by his expertise in markmenship. Robert placed various targets at alternating distances across the fence of the field. Robert fired rapidly, mowing them down with precision. Young Quaid watched in awe of his uncle, the priest, handling the deadly weapon like a jewler cut diamonds. After striking all the targets, Robert turned to see young Quaid gasping at the site of the destruction. Calmly, Robert addressed him.

"Jacob, as much as we are to see the good in all people, evil exists everywhere."

Robert hesitated, then turned and holstered his gun. He continued.

"God created them both, good and evil; just as He created the strong and the weak. However, it is not for the strong to conquer. It is their divine responsibility to defend the weak. So must it be; that good combat evil. Thus, to ignore the presence of evil is to become as evil itself. Remember your Romans, Jacob. 'Be not overcome of evil, but overcome evil with good.'"[5]

Young Quaid nodded in the affirmative. He looked up and asked, "Uncle, was my father also good with a gun?"

"Why yes," replied Robert.

"He was very adroit with all short range weaponry. He was superior in the use of the battle axe, and the blades, but he was equally skilled with revolver, rifle, and the bow." Robert continued. "Your father had a kind of blind fury when it came to war. Such a rage I have never seen. It was a controlled anger; directed and precise."

Young Quaid knew little of his father's past. He could recall the years spent on the family farm. Young Quaid could still

---

5   Holy Bible - Romans 12:21

remember how his father spoke to him. It was always with kindness and understanding. He was a man of patience. The elder Quaid addressed young Quaid with respect, despite the fact he was his child. His father gave him many insights. Those lessons, young Quaid fondly remembered. He could recall that bear of a man cradling him like a baby and carrying him upon his back. His father's affection poured out of every inch of his being. That is what young Quaid remembered. This current revelation was not anything like the father he knew.

"Uncle," asked young Quaid, "when my father fought in the war, did he kill many men?"

"Jacob," Robert replied, "your father's thoughts and prayers are his. It is not my place to divulge these actions which he sought not to reveal."

Young Quaid bowed his head shamefully. Robert placed his arm around him.

"Jacob, you have much work to do," said Robert. "And many days of practice ahead. I know you will develop your talent such that your father would be proud."

Young Quaid looked up and smiled. Robert took his big, rough hand and shook the top of young Quaid's head of hair as if scrubbing a floor.

"Jacob," Robert continued. "I know a man who can help you. Next month we will pay him a visit."

Young Quaid's exuberance abounded. As the saddening thoughts of his lost father slowly faded, he resumed his practice.

Evenings were devoted to faith. Young Quaid learned from Robert to have a strong faith in God and his laws. Being a man of higher education, Robert had many connections to all branches of learning. Young Quaid benefited from these acquaintances. From these, young Quaid developed a line of reasoning and deduction; a form of function that would serve him in the future.

On the first Saturday of each month, Robert and Jacob would venture to the university to listen to the great orators of the time. Young Quaid thoroughly enjoyed these visits. They sparked his interest to know more. Young Quaid absorbed more, and more, and more knowledge. From mathematics, to letters, to philosophy, he assimilated them all. His favorite classification of erudition was music. Oh, how beautiful it was! He loved the elegant instruments with their refined grace. The soothing sounds and dramatic overtures, took young Quaid to places only realized in his dreams.

Young Quaid recalled a trip to the city and its opera house. The statuesque stone structure appeared to leap out into the boulevard. Like a good novel, the façade did not begin to tell what lay inside. The appearance was as a fortress, looming in the distance. It stood as if to warn those who dare try to breach the entrance, of the many perils that await inside. Despite the portentous construct, harbingers of horse and carriage came carrying patrons round and round. They tarried, then would move on like a merry-go-round come to life. Participants would exit the four wheeled wagons of wonder and make haste for the door. Each member wore the current trappings of high society. The women in their long, flowing, flowery frocks, with parasol in hand; walked by. Each lady was adorned with a fluffy framed hat. As they moved, the headdresses would appear to dance.

The gentlemen wore a bland mix of grey and black. Only a solitary splash of white from their shirts seemed to break up the monotony of those colorless clothes. Each tie was classy but dull. Most were topped off with a tall hat.

As you entered, the ceilings rose up as if to pierce the sky. Not every cloud had a silver lining, mostly because the dome was adorned with gold. Gold was as far as the eye could see. Deep red drapes flowed over the arched passageways. It was like looking at a living Christmas present. Columns of support sprung up throughout. Each had flowers which lay in the stone. At the top was an angel. With harp in hand, the cheerful cherub appeared ready to play at a given notice. On the many walls, horses that fly were powerfully pulling carriages. The wings were so wide it was if they could glide right off the surface. Big cats were cast with great strength; they had teeth that could tear, and eyes that scared the souls of those who dared to stare into them. The serpent's smooth scales surrounded the statuesque supports like shackles. What grace! What majesty! What beauty was this? Still this was not what the people had come for.

Young Quaid and his uncle proceeded down the aisle past numerous onlookers. Each had become accustomed to their seat. Patiently, the mass of human packaging awaited the first note. Young Quaid and Robert sat down. They adjusted their body's position so that nothing could deter them from the full frontal musical force. The waiting became like an aphrodisiac. Young Quaid had a nervousness about him. It was a controlled excitement. Robert appeared relaxed and readied for something miraculous.

There was a tapping. The crowd grew hush. Lights slowly dimmed over the stage. Then, it struck. The orchestra hit the opening chord. It resounded out across the ocean of humanity like a wave. It ended in a crash of symbols. Without hearing a single word, Robert could infer young Quaid's approval. The first actor moved forward onto the dimly lit stage. She opened her mouth, and it seemed to the boy that the heavens had opened with it. What joy! What sounds! What wondrous noise! Young Quaid tingled from the top of his head to the tip of his toes. Surely only God himself had ever heard such beauty and power in one presence. To percieve such sounds must only be for the Most High. Young Quaid looked up at his uncle, still in awe. This was a gift that love lends to a fortunate few.

Young Quaid never forgot that day, or the other times they returned to the opera. To Quaid, the boundless beauty of song never died. It grew in his heart and spilled over into his being. His being loved. It was the love of God. It was the love of God's law. Quaid loved the law, lived the law, became the law. Yes, Jacob Quaid had been seeded, tended, and harvested in God's law. He was like a tree.

Chapter 2

The day was hot. It was the kind of hot that felt like there was a melding connection between earth and sun. The heat could be seen rising from the terra, in waves. The rippling of the air above the ground created a dreamworld. In the sky, of that one western town, there were no clouds. No evidence of moisture from which the sands could drink. The arid west wind blew, but the breeze brought no relief. What it did blow in was trouble.

The clink of metal spurs struck the hardwood of the walk on the storefronts. Boots, heavily laden with dust of past dry days walked in a uniform pattern. As the sun blazed down, the boots marched closer to their destination. Clink clank. Clink clank. Clink clank.

Clink clank went the mechanical pairs of spurs striking down on the wooden path below. The echo resounded. There was no hesitation, as the vibrations passed storefront after storefront. No break in step. The rhythmic sound intensified with the passing of each stern structure. No pause, as the pitch passed the grocer. Clink clank. Clink clank. Clink clank. No interruption, as the audible metal reached the diner. Clink clank. Clink clank. Clink clank. No stopping, as the stride of purpose moved past the physician's residence. Clink clank. Clink clank. Clink clank. The repetitious noise moved steadily on, by the undertaker, the hotel, and the saloon. Clink clank. Clink clank. Clink clank. The metronome pattern continued through the streets right up to the entrance of the town's bank.

An all quiet sounded. The firing of steel heels encircled the fortified ingress. Seconds passed as if hours without a single metallic tone. As one looked up, you could see the large brick building, two stories high. The windows were covered by thick iron bars like a jailhouse. The wood and metal meshed like armor. Small green shutters adorned them in an attempt to downplay the ominous sight. Thick mortar-filled walls covered the space on all sides. It was crushed out like frosting flowing from a layered cake. The bank was an impenetrable box jutting out from the main causeway like a thumb. The sun shone on it but cast a dark, gloomy shadow. One would think it could come alive as the wind bellowed across its surface like a carrion cry. In front, a large black sign rose above the wooden double doors. The doors stood strong, tall, and daunting like a totem pole. Adorned on them were two large ring shaped handles. Superior to that was engraved large block letters, white and full. It read BANK. Inside that barrier was the sum of the town's peoples sweat, toil, and tears. More than paper and coin, it contained the raw materials of imagination. The future lay within. It was possibility, growth, travel, and adventure. All manner of desirability had been stored up in savings. It held the savings of lifetimes. It held the savings of money.

The all quiet lingered like words on the tip of the tongue. Then came a crashing bang. Boots burst through the threshold. The hold-up was on.

The cowboys were clothed in tattered attire. Dust covered their boots. They wore worn shirts and vests that had faded by exposure to wind, sun, and sand. The hats were pulled down firmly above each furrowed brow, covering the lines which were etched into their foreheads. The bandits completed their garb with a kerchief. Tied around each nose and mouth, it only left the scowl of their darkened eyes. Guns were drawn and at the ready. The cowboys burst onto the scene as a collective gasp arose from the floor of the bank. One teller looked up from his visor to see the long grey coats which were once the sign of the Confederacy, staring back at him.

The interior of the bank was not well lit. Bathed in yellow bands of sunshine, the patrons glowed. Each particulate illuminated the smoothly sanded wood walls. Like chocolate, they appeared solid, yet soft. Full bodied in height, they stemmed up to a coffered ceiling. It was like a maze. A pattern perfection of an elongated labyrinth lay above their heads.

The tellers stood behind a stronghold counter that covered one-third of the room. There were small gaps between the raised lip of the counter. In each gap stood a teller, with pen and paper in hand. Small gold lamps with tinted green glass tops, garnished the work space.

In the stunned silence, a teller peered into the gun barrels, which seemed to grow larger with each minute. The room began spinning; one, two, three times. Another banker tried to quickly count the adversaries; two, four, six, cowboys. Too many guns, with too many patrons present; this would not allow for any attempt at resistance. The two guards were caught unaware. They would have no chance at survival at this close range, out manned and outgunned. They held their ground reluctantly. The patrons were still. Icebound and barely breathing, they were afraid to move. Every civilian knew of the existence of outlaws but no one expected to see them present in their town, raiding their bank. Some tried to withdraw into the shadowy corners of the building, making their appearance seem small and unassuming. Beads of sweat began to roll down a tellers face. A bitter taste came up in the back of his throat as one of the cowboys exclaimed, "All the money, now!"

Sensing the teller's apprehension, the cowboy looked past his comrades and stepped forward toward the banker. His eyes burned with a fury. The firey red spheres burst as the sun. The flash was as if to incinerate the choroid coat right off the retina. One again, he shouted, "All the money, now!"

During his approach, the cowboy felt that something was amiss. It was more than the morose money changers. It was bigger than the besieged bankers. It was not the numbness of the air. A panic fell over the cowboy as sudden as a curtain being dropped. Quickly, the cowboy spun around, brandishing his weapon in an attempt to foil any attempt at force. None came.

With his mind still reeling, the cowboy began to count. Intellect now intact, the cowboy whispered across his lips,

"One, two, three, four, five,....six!"

There were one too many hats, one too many masks, one too many guns. All were drawn and trained on each other! Who was who? In this frantic moment, there were no assurances.

Five men had organized. Five men had planned. Five men had executed the heist. Five men had arrived to this point. Now, six men stood. Six men were silent. Six men were still. Six men were starring, starring down at six six-guns.

In that instant in time, the other cowboys became aware of their plight. Sweat dripped from their faces. As their hands began to tremble, their voices rang out in succession.

"Don't move!" one cowboy exclaimed.

"Give it up!" shouted another.

"Drop your weapon!" screamed a third.

Shockingly, to the left of the ring leader, a shot rang out. Then another volley sounded. A third blast came before an overwhelming "Stop!" silenced the battery.

Smoke from the gunfire filled the air like a fog. The smell of flint burned the nostrils. Each eye watered from the visible vapor. Puddles of red blood rose forth from the floor. Three bandits now lay lifeless on the wood. The reflection of death spilled up as each cowboy looked down. Now, there were only three.

Each cowboy took a long poised look at each other. Each tried desperately to discern friend from foe. Slowly, methodically, the hammers of the cowboy's weapons were pulled back. Three clicks sounded from three hands. Three sets of eyes were all looking for some sign from the trinity.

Suddenly, a new sound arose. It came up quickly. The sound seemed familiar. It was the sound of claws scratching the floor, as four legs raced towards them. It was accompanied with a low-pitched growl. The growl grew more powerful with each moment. At the door was a shadow. A long figure emerged. A lone gray wolf stood with eyes wide. He was large, standing almost three feet at the shoulder. The length was approximately six feet from nose to tail. He was grey, with brown accents on the ears, shoulders, and legs. The fur appeared rough. It stood up and out as if to reach towards its prey. The wolf had its back arched and front legs apart, ready to strike. The ears were up high. From the mouth of black came white razor teeth. As he snarled, you could see the small amount of pink gum just above the dark dot that was his nose. Behind the long snoot were piercing golden-green eyes, with furrows between them, displaying his anger. The posture was protective, and strong.

The cowboys were in awe, but not in shock. Their extensive military training had not been wasted. Their band of bandits had done their intelligence gathering. Each cowboy was well aware of the town's Marshall and his unique companion. This nature's predator was the Marshall's friend and partner.

The tale of the carnivorous herald had been picked up and relayed to the money poachers. They knew that a wolf cub had been given to the young Marshall as a boy. The stories of their exploits had been well known to all the town's people, and in the cities beyond its borders.

One such instance saw the very young Quaid riding through a dense desert terrain. Young Quaid's mount trotted through the burning sands with Poe in tandem. The wolf cub ran parallel, twisting and turning through the sandy brush and rock. The wild beast instinctively avoided the large strides of the ungulate horse. His nose was up, eyes front, and the ears were elevated to perceive. Young Quaid could feel the breeze flow freely through the locks of curly hair tucked under his hat.

The young lad proceeded hastily up a sharp incline of stone. The shoes of his horse clapped loudly all the way up the elevation. All those rocks and bushes had provided pockets of protection for predators to escape view. Once the ridge was breeched, young Quaid's steed came to a full and complete stop.

The horse reared. The boy was flung from the saddle like a stone from a sling. Young Quaid was hurled awkwardly off the side like so much excess baggage. He landed hard, striking the right side of his torso. Stunned, yet still mentally aware, the young man glanced forward to see what had spooked his ride. Now, at eye level, young Quaid regarded a viper coiled and ready to strike. It was long, brown, and appeared checkered, as a gaming table. A strange rattling noise bit the air. The lad looked directly into the diamond-shaped eyes slanted ever so slightly behind the raised nostrils. Two long fangs dropped down below the gums. Shiny white, razor sharp, and with a hint of moisture from the venom, the teeth shone the light as a sunburst. The split tongue was spit out repeatedly, perceiving. Sweaty and scared, young Quaid was transfixed. The boy froze.

Seeing his human brother in danger, the young man's companion did not hesitate. The muscles of the wolf cub came into sync, as if aligned as the planets. The wolf ran and leapt in a solitary motion. At that moment, there was no wind, no sound. Poe's incisors bounded forward, grasping the reptile by the neck. The steely knives drove into the head of the snake, exploding into the skull. A large popping pushed out red blood, splattering young Quaid's face.

This power and precision of execution was not missed by the cowboys. They were well aware of the Marshall's arsenal of protection. The Marshall was an adapt tactician, but his partner added an air of unpredictability. The cowboys knew if the wolf was here, so was the Marshall. This would explain a lot.

The wolf began to slowly circle. Every head was on a swivel. The ring leader knew that the wolf would strike an enemy at any moment. The eyes of the cowboys patiently followed the beast's path. This would be the ring leader's chance. Once the wolf attacked, he would unleash a ballistic barrage, ending the standoff. The wolf continued to circle to the left, towards the bank counter. His fangs drew down, as his snarl drew deep. The canine crouched, then leapt. Across twelve feet of floor flew the fury. Down went the cowboy under the weight of thylacine thunder. The ring leader turned and faced the last standing cowboy. As he pivoted, he opened fire, unloading all chambers into the opposing cowboy. Bang! Bang! Bang! Bang! Bang! The smoke flamed, as the hammer sparked the cartridge. The chest of his opponent exploded like a red pyrotechnic display. The cowboy dropped to his knees, and as a last rush of air was exhaled, he fell like timber. Down and out, his eyes became transfixed. The kerchief was bloodied. Then the red liquid slowly dripped to the floor.

The ring leader paused, straightened his reserve, and approached his kill with a smug smile. A glorified gleam sparkled in his eyes. The cowboy lowered his gun so that he could inspect his work. Relaxed, the ring leader strode over and knelt down.

The cowboy started to pull back the mask so that he could see the dying face of the Marshall. He wanted him to know just who had beaten him. The cowboy wanted to savor the moment of triumph over this puny impudent lawman; this insignificant insect. He stretched out his arm and his hand reached toward the fallow face. A loud click, clapped in the cowboy's ear. The turning tumbler of a colt revolver had been realized. The cowboy felt the pressure of a barrel on the back of his neck. Turning his gaze, but not moving a muscle, the cowboy could see the wolf at his feet. There was no body lying on the floor behind him. A sick feeling came over the bandit. His nausea was the realization that the gray wolf had struck at his master, thus leaving his accomplice to be riddled by bullets from his own gun.

Four bodies now lay oblong on the floor. A gun at his back, the cowboy was helpless. The erect Marshall pulled down his kerchief.

"You are under arrest, Mister," he said.

"Come now, and no more blood will need to be spilled."

The captive cowboy relented and rose. His shoulders slunk in defeat. The Marshall directed him to the door with a flick of his firearm. The cowboy began to tread slowly. Under his breath, the cowboy spitefully said,

"They were my friends!"

The Marshall hearing his words responded,

"'They that live by the sword, shall die by the sword.'"[6]

---

6   Holy Bible - Matthew 26:52

CHAPTER 3

Crash! The heavy metal collided, as the jail cell door was flung closed. Looking around; the walls were of stone, thick stone. It was cold, hard, damp, and dark in the barred confinement. No comforts. Furnishings were spartan. A single cot, and a solitary wooden table were arranged on opposite sides of the cell. A small stool was tucked underneath the table. The table had two large buckets resting on its surface. One held drinking water, the other was for waste. This was all that this tomb contained. It had a high ceiling. No real window was present, at least not one that you could contemplate climbing through. This was no playground. No happiness could be found here. Only barren desperation could be heard emanating from the stark surroundings.

A total of four rooms made up the cell block. There was an anteroom which doubled as the Marshall's work place. A desk, files, supplies, and guns filled the space. The floor, like the walls, again was cold stone. All the hard surfaces were kept clean, however. Like a cave, the only light came through the small opening at the front door. Covered with thick bars, one could hardly call it a window. When the front door of the jail was opened, light flooded into the darkness like water running down hill. It was bleak, but what lay ahead for its inhabitants was markedly more discouraging.

The Marshall's desk was covered with papers, ink, and pens. It was one isle of clutter in the desert of this domain. A large gun rack held multiple weapons; knives, an axe, rifles, handguns, and even a sword. The rack was located just behind the Marshall's chair. The chair was wood but a complicated creation. It had the ability to swivel and roll. Hand rests were mounted to each side, and the back was girded with interrupted straps of metal attached to the wood frame. It was much too prominent for a man of the Marshall's simple tastes.

From this house, a prisoner could be sent to a federal court where he would stand before a judge. Judges, in this part of the country, did not take well to bank robbers, horse thieves, or murderers. Justice was served swiftly. It was not in Quaid's nature to judge. Quaid upheld the law. He left it in God's hands to impose judgment. Quaid believed, as was written in Amos,

'Let judgment run down as waters, and righteousness as a mighty stream.'[7]

Sitting in his chair in the anteroom, Quaid heard the prisoner cry out.

"Hey, Marshall! What's taking so long?" the prisoner shouted.

---

7   Holy Bible - Amos 5:24

As Quaid peered in the cell, he could see the prisoner supine on the cot. His feet were resting on the bars. His hat was half tipped forward covering his eyes. A dim-witted grin gleamed across his face.

"What do you require?" asked Quaid.

"Require?" responded the prisoner.

"I require nothing." Then a pause.

"I merely would like to give you some advice."

"Advice? From you?" retorted Quaid.

After a time, Quaid continued sarcastically, "Well certainly, sir. I have always, been eager to learn."

"You know Marshall you might just want to release me." Quaid glared at him in disbelief. The prisoner continued, "I would not want to be here when my friends come calling," Quaid quipped quickly back, "I will notify the undertaker." The prisoner leapt to his feet, angered. The grin was gone. It was replaced by a hard scowl. The prisoner's tone had changed. Without a blink, he starred full into Quaid's stern green globes. Swearing, the prisoner responded, "Hell, you don't know the half of it Marshall."

"Enlighten me," responded Quaid. The prisoner turned from the face to face confrontation. His posture relaxed as he reclined back onto the cot.

"Why spoil the party?" said the prisoner smiling as if knowing the climax before the start of the play. The prisoner continued, "I just want to be there to see 'em blow out the candles."

There was a long contemplative pause, as Quaid looked past the prisoner's dark brown eyes into his soul. Neither man moved. The silence broke as the prisoner again spoke.

"You see Marshall, the Friends of the South will come for me, mark my words."

"Friends of the South?" questioned Quaid.

"Have you not known that the war between the states is over? It has been, for years now," said Quaid.

"Tell that to my horsemen in grey, Marshall," the prisoner responded, with an air of contempt.

Just then, the Marshall heard the front door of the jailhouse being thrown open. The heavy wood struck the inside wall with a loud thud. Quaid reeled around quickly, grasping his gun. His eyes focused frantically in an effort to determine the source of this hastened entrance.

"Marshall! Marshall Quaid!" exclaimed a high pitched voice. It rang out like the toll of a bell, and the echo could be heard resounding throughout the structure of stone.

"Come quick! Come quick now!"continued the distraught diction. Quaid strode forward into the anteroom with the power of purpose. There in front of him stood young Patrick O'Riley. Patrick was small and fragile-looking. His skin was pale. He had light hair with a hint of red. Freckles adorned his face, and stood out like ink on a blotter. But, his countenance did not display frivolity. Patrick was flush. His forehead was wrinkled and his eyes moved a bit sporadically. Quaid easily recognized the panic, not only in his voice, but the nervous anxiety of the lad's posture. Poor little Patrick was only a little bit over ten years old, and a little bit over four feet tall. Quaid was acutely aware of the height difference. So, to alleviate some of the tension of the apprehensive encounter, Quaid bent down to one knee to address the lad.

"What is it Patty?" Quaid asked.

"There is a scary stranger playing poker at Dad's place." Patrick was the son of Sean O'Reilly, the proprietor of the town's saloon.

"Sorry, son," Quaid replied. "There is no law against playing poker."

Patrick paused, "This man... this man is different," Patrick stuttered.

"How so?" asked Quaid.

Patrick gathered himself, took a deep breath, then started, "He is as big as a house. He is bigger than you, and dark. But not just in his face, he is all dressed in grey and black."

"Grey," Quaid whispered under his breath. Quaid's mind began to extrapolate. Could this be the 'Friends of the South' that the prisoner had spoken of? What other possible business could this stranger be involved in? Quaid continued to think deeply. Should he barrel in with his gun drawn? Perhaps he should be more deliberate, evaluate the situation first? Patrick continued,

"He has been there all day, not moving. It is like he is waiting for something, something evil."

Quaid stood erect. He adjusted his holster, checked his firearm, and tapped on his belt knife. Then Quaid walked around his desk and reached for a rifle from the rack. Quaid straightened his hat and made for the door. Lastly, Quaid turned, and cried out, "Poe protect!"

A large gray wolf, hidden, now darted from the room. Then out the door the wolf blew as in a puff of smoke.

Poe had been Quaid's protector for years. Quaid could still visualize the vicissitude of the day his father reached into his pack and produced the young cub. The then young Quaid's grin went from ear to ear. He hugged the soft bundle, and held him tight against his body. He thought he would never let go. Love does that. Love changes a person. Finally, boy and beast both knew love. 'There is no fear in love, but perfect love casts out fear,' [8] young Quaid had thought. From that day forward, there were no more worries.

Back at the jailhouse, Quaid gathered his thoughts, and looked down to address Patrick.

"Come on Patty, let us go pay a visit to your man in grey and black."

Quaid sensed the boy's dread. Quaid stopped and took a step back. Quaid looked again at Patrick and smiled.

"Evil, huh?" Quaid said jokingly.

"Remember Patty, 'Judge not, that ye be not judged.'"[9]

Quaid contemplated the words as they rolled over his lips. They were simple and true. Quaid cleared his mind and again addressed Patrick.

"Did you happen to speak with him,?"

As Quaid spoke to Patrick, he reached out and opened the door. Stepping out onto the wooden planks of the front walk, Patrick replied, "No sir."

After a few seconds, Patrick continued,

"I was afraid."

Quaid squinted into the white hot sunlight. He turned and faced the young man, blocking its radiance. Quaid peered

---

8   Holy Bible - I John 4:18
9   Holy Bible - Matthew 7:1

directly into the boys eyes. He placed both of his rugged hands on the boy's shoulders.

"Listen Patty," Quaid started.

"I am going to tell you something my father told me when I was your age."

Patrick held motionless.

"He said, Jacob, do not fear any man, ... fear only God. 'And fear not them which kill the body, but are not able to kill the soul. Rather fear him which is able to destroy both soul and body.'"[10]

Patrick hung his head. He felt ashamed. But as the words of wisdom enveloped him, his spirit became lifted. Patrick raised his head back up, revealing a large smile.

"I understand, Marshall," said Patrick.

"Now then Patty," said Quaid

"Let us go together to meet this man in grey and black."

Quaid took Patrick's hand in his, and they strode across the dirt and sand street. There was no hesitation until they reached the saloon. Quaid stood at the swinging doors. He could hear music rising above the chatter. Voices of partisans carried across the large room as each patron engaged in his favorite form of extracurricular activity. Nothing unusual for O'Reilly's, Quaid thought. Quaid took a deep breath, squeezed Patrick's hand tight, and stepped through the double doors.

It was a whole new world. Tables were full of men in various stages of inebriation. Glasses and bottles were strewn all over the tables and bar. The only areas not covered were where the

---

10   Holy Bible - Matthew 10:28

gamblers were engaged in cards. A few men stood, slung over the bar, as the bartender went efficiently about his tasks.

The bar was poorly lit. It was dry and dusty, like the town's main road. Scattered throughout the islands of self service, the men sat, talked, laughed, gamed and reveled. Every man's attire was distinct. From formal to informal, neck tie to kerchiefs, spotless to earth covered; were the occupants. Quaid quickly scanned from front to back. His vision panned the entire room, looking for his man. No one seemed to even realize that the Marshall had entered. Those parked at the bar did not look up. The remainder proceeded with whatever it was they were doing in a manner equally oblivious to Quaid's eminent entrance.

The Marshall spotted his quarry at a back corner table. He was a hulk in black. The stranger looked grim. His hat concealed his face. A shadow covered the rest of his form. Patrick was right. This man had more shades of grey and black than the caverns of hell. Quaid could not see the face but the attire was distinctive. The stranger wore a long dark grey coat. It had long sleeves, a folded lapel, and black buttons down the center. It was so long it draped over his massive frame and almost touched the floor. From under the hanging coat came large black boots, with steel spurs, thick heels, and fully rounded leather toes. Behind the coat you could see a black shirt with large black buttons. It was collared and stiff. Everything else about the stranger was mired in a murky mystery.

Quaid took a breath to clear his thoughts. Quaid traveled back to his studies as a young boy. Ephesians came to mind.

'For we wrestle not against flesh and blood, but against principalities, against powers, against the rulers of the darkness of this world.' [11]

Quaid confidently strode forth. All the while, Quaid looked for signs that there may be others. More cowboys could be waiting, watching; contemplating violence. Men like this, men of evil, never worked alone. As Quaid's gait quickened he recalled the country of Gadarenes. 'And he answered, saying, "My name is legion for we are many."'[12] Quaid's peripheral vision went out, as he drew near to the stranger's table. Quaid let go of Patrick's hand, as he may require its use to defend himself. Each step Quaid took mounded the pressure. Quaid felt the tingle of tension on the raised hairs of his neck. Quaid glared deeply at the man in grey and black. His right hand held his cards, the left was wrapped as if injured. Quaid could see no visible weapon. It all seemed so suspicious. Quaid, however, was an officer of the peace. He would not resort to force unless the law required it.

At present, the Marshall stood over his target, The stranger in grey and black held fast. No movement. He did not even look up. Quaid wondered if he was even breathing. The Marshall decided to make the first move.

"So stranger, are you just passing through?" asked Quaid.

The man was frozen. His countenance was unchanged by Quaid's inquiry. Then after what seemed like hours of silence, he spoke...

"I am on the road to Emmaus."

"Emmaus?" Quaid questioned. The Marshall continued.

---

11   Holy Bible - Ephesians 6:12
12   Holy Bible - Mark 5:9

"I do not believe I have heard of that town."

Without moving a muscle, the stranger replied, "I am confident that you have, Marshall."

Quaid became somewhat lost in thought. The name did sound vaguely familiar. For some reason, Quaid could just not recall from where. Quaid's mind continued on his memory quest. He knew that he had not visited that place before, yet, something about what the stranger said rang true. Quaid decided to take another angle.

"Well, sir, do you have a name?"

The gargoyle-like figure, motionless, responded, "Yes."

Quaid waited on bent ear. No more sounds slipped from the mouth of the massive man. Quaid shifted his weight, then said, "Well stranger, may I ask what it is?"

"Black." He said calmly.

"Mr. Black, it has been a real pleasure conversing with you," Quaid replied.

"And may I add," Quaid continued, "that I hope your travels will be, uneventful."

With that, Quaid turned and started to walk away. He sensed nothing from behind, nothing from across the room, and nothing from the bar. As Quaid headed toward the door he addressed Sean O'Reilly standing behind the bar.

"Do not worry about this one, Sean. He is simply passing through."

With that, Quaid made his way toward the exit. He again forced his way between the hinged doors. Quaid stepped out of the dark and onto the burning sands of the main street.

CHAPTER 4

It was late afternoon on a Monday. The sun had already begun its descent, painting the desert canyon with pastels. The ambient warmth bathed Quaid as he strolled down an empty street. The solitary soul strode slowly but not aimlessly. Feeling the need to talk, Quaid turned towards the town's chapel. Quaid was a regular on Sunday morning, and often on Saturday evening as well. His faith was strong. Practice makes perfect, and this also applied to prayer. Quaid's pattern of dedication to prayer had begun early under his mother and father's teachings. His tutorage continued with his uncle, the ordained minister, Robert. As Quaid grew in height, he grew in faith. And as his uncle was so found of saying,'The effectual fervent prayer of a righteous man availeth much.'[13]

As Quaid approached the steps of the church he glanced up at the steeple piercing the evening sky. The orange darts

---

13   Holy Bible - James 5:16

careened around the wooden obelisk. Quaid made his way up the steps to the front door. As he drew open the large framed barrier, an unusual feeling came over him. It was from his earlier encounter with the stranger. The sound of the stranger's voice, his stature and style, it all seemed hauntingly familiar. Even the stranger's words still echoed through Quaid's mind. "I am on the road to Emmaus." Quaid began searching; searching for answers. He knew where to look for guidance; God's house.

Quaid entered the chapel as the last bit of daylight poured through the stained glass like a rainbow. At the alter was a holy man kneeling in prayer. His back was directed towards Quaid, yet the Marshall could still percieve the murmur of his supplication.

"I believe in God, the Father Almighty, Creator of heaven and earth; and in Jesus Christ. His only son, our Lord; who was conceived by the Holy Spirit, born of the virgin Mary, suffered under Pontius Pilot, was crucified, died and was buried. He descended into hell; the third day He arose again from the dead. He ascended into heaven, sitteth at the right hand of God the Father Almighty; from hence He shall come to judge the living and the dead. I believe in the Holy Spirit, the holy church, the communion of saints, the forgiveness of sins, the resurrection of the body, and life everlasting. Amen."

Quaid continued forward, but cautiously as not to disturb. The padre percieved the approach. The gentleman, quickly made the sign of the cross, stood, and turned to face his guest. The vestment he wore was white. It covered the coffee-colored cassock like cream. The standard surplice was no surprise to Quaid; in fact, in a way, it was reassuring.

The father's face was full, being well fed. Lines crossed his forehead, sprung out from the orbits, and drained down from his nose to his chin. The hair of the pastor was mostly grey, with a hint of youth dwelling deep at the follicle. The filaments, lacking fullness, gave the fibers a flimsy form. It was combed, not unkempt. Staring into his eyes, Quaid could see a spark, an essence of the divine, blazing behind each dark pupil. The smile was one of restraint. The poised pursed expression curled one corner of his mouth. There was joy here, Quaid thought; genuine joy. The affect spread out from his features and enveloped Quaid like a warm blanket.

"Jacob, how may I be of service?" he asked.

"I would very much like to talk," Quaid replied.

"Should we step over to the confessional?" he said "'If we confess our sins, he is faithful and just to forgive us our sins, and to cleanse us from all unrighteousness'"[14]

"No, thanks, father," Quaid said.

"My sins are great but I need the ears of a friend."

"Certainly Jacob," he replied.

Quaid knew what he wanted to say but did not know exactly where to begin. The clergyman sensed Quaid's apprehension. Slowly, he motioned with his hand, then said,

"Shall we sit down, then, Jacob?"

Quaid sat himself down in the first pew. The priest then lowered himself next to him.

"Now Jacob, what is this visit all about?" he asked.

"Well father," Quaid replied. "I have been troubled by a recent event. It all revolves around a short confrontation with

---

14   Holy Bible - I John 1:9

a stranger in grey and black." Quaid stopped, and gathered his thoughts. "I was asked by little Patrick O'Reilly to come down to the saloon to inquire about a stranger. When I gazed upon this man in grey and black, an unsettling feeling came over me."

"What did it feel like?" asked the priest.

"It was a feeling of dread, father. Like I was a little boy, about to be punished," said Quaid.

The priest nodded, then said, "Go on."

"When I engaged him in conversation, I asked him where he was heading. He told me, 'to Emmaus.'"

The priest's eyes widened. Quaid saw the look of surprise spread across the father's face. Not waiting for the priest to respond, Quaid asked, "What does this mean?" No answer came. Quaid continued, "The stranger seemed to think I would know." Another long pause struck the two, as the silence lit up the front alter. The priest reached over and opened his bible to Luke. He began to read. "'And, behold, two of them went that same day to a village called Emmaus which was from Jerusalem about threescore furlongs. And they talked together of all these things which had happened. And it came to pass, that while they communed together and reasoned, Jesus himself drew near, and went with them. But their eyes were holden that they should not know him.'"[15] The padre closed the book and turned toward Quaid. "Jacob, it refers to the Gospels. Our Lord appeared on the road to Emmaus, but he was not recognized by his companions. In some form or another, you must know this stranger. And like these travelers in the Gospels, you failed to recognize him."

---

15   Holy Bible - Luke 24:13

Quaid's face went blank. He looked off to one side so that his mind could soak up what his ears had just heard. As Quaid processed the preist's perception, his memory shifted back through the years to his childhood. He pictured himself growing up. He remembered a boy running through the forest; playing on rocks, and spending time in the kitchen with his mother. Then, he saw the tragic loss of his father in a barn fire.

Young Quaid was asleep that night. Resting comfortably in the loft above the main room, he was awoken by the sound of rushing feet and the crashing of the front door. Startled, the young Quaid leapt out of bed and climbed down the ladder of the loft with haste. Skipping the last step, he jumped down and firmly planted both feet on the ground with a thud. Young Quaid turned quickly and ran to the front window. The night sky was full ablaze. That blaze came from the barn. It was full on fire. The conflagrant flames towered up engulfing the structure like an octopus' tentacles swallowing its prey.

Young Quaid scanned around the front of the burning barn. Red, yellow, and blue danced over the dwelling, reflecting in the boy's eyes. There at the main door stood his father, Matthan. A sudden pain struck the boy as he watched the events unfold. Young Quaid rushed out the front of the house. At the top of his voice he screamed, "Pappy!" The elder Quaid spun and looked upon his young child racing towards him as fast as his legs could carry him. Tears were streaming down his face. As young Quaid reached his father's position, he again let out a breathless yell, "Pappy, no!"

His father reached out his arms and grasped young Quaid's shoulders. He then bent down to one knee to look young Quaid in the eye.

"Jacob," he said. "I need to go in there and free the horses, otherwise they will perish. Do not worry son, I will be fine."

Young Quaid responded, "Let me help."

"No." said the elder. "Fire is a dangerous foe, unpredictable in its advance. I must go in alone." His father paused, looked toward the barn, then looked back at his son.

"I want you to round up Angel and Demon after I set them free. They will likely run, being afraid. I want you to corral them. Can you do that for me son?"

"Yes," replied young Quaid.

"Isaiah said it best, 'Fear thou not for I am with thee. Be not dismayed, for I am thy God. I will strengthen thee; yea, I will help thee; yea, I will uphold thee with the right hand of my righteousness,'"[16] said the elder.

With that Matthan Quaid rose, and headed for the barn door. He lifted the bar lock and threw it to the side in one motion. Matthan Quaid had been blessed with great strength, a gift he had used often in the past. He could feel the imposing heat generated from behind the door. Undaunted, he grasped the handle and threw it open. The elder Quaid pivoted and glanced back at his son. He nodded, then disappeared.

Young Quaid waited. It seemed like hours. Then, through the vibrating yellow and red waves came a white hot figure, galloping. She was tall, strong, and majestic. She came striding out of the pyre like a bullet shot out of a gun. Young Quaid

---

16   Holy Bible - Isaiah 41:10

saw the image and cried out, "Angel!" She came to a stop, then trotted directly over to young Quaid. The boy placed his hand on her nose.

"Good girl," he said. Angel was a gorgeous white quarter horse, about fifteen hands high. Her proportions were perfect. The length of her head equaled the distance from the point of hock to the fold of stifle. Her depth of girth and the fold of stifle to the croup, were also the same. Yes, she was magnificent. From behind, as young Quaid circled, he could see the vertical lines pass straight upward from the centers of the fetlocks through the points of hock, to the points of the rear. Angel was a beauty. But, beyond her perfect stature, she could run. She ran as light travelled across the sky. Aside from speed, this perfect pony could cut. Angel had it all, agility, velocity, power, and balance. She had one more quality no other horse had, grace. It was a God given grace.

A loud explosion broke Quaid's concentration. He turned back toward the barn. Before his eyes, young Quaid saw the structure disintegrate, walls and all.

"No!" shouted young Quaid.

"No, no, no, no...No!" He ran as quickly as he could bear his weight, right up to the entrance of the barn. The heat pushed him back, as he shielded his face with his arm. The bright light reflected against the dark black sky. His tears flowed like a river. The sorrow swelled up in his soul. Such pain he had never felt. The discomfort burned his stomach, and ate through him all the way down to his knees. He became weak and dropped to the ground in defeat. Kneeling, young Quaid reared his head to the heavens, and while weeping, exclaimed, "Pappy!"

Young Quaid covered his face with his hands. He could not bear to witness the destruction and loss any longer. His grief overwhelmed him. He sat, sobbing. Now, it was completely quiet, not the way a war hero should leave this world. There was no fanfare, no spoken word, nothing to mark the passing. Young Quaid could not bring himself to his feet. He stayed down.

Finally, the front door of the house sprung open and young Quaid's mother came rushing forth.

"Jacob!" she yelled. "Are you hurt?"

Young Quaid raised his face from out of his hands and replied, "No."

His mother fell on him, in tears.

"Jacob, it's O.K."

Young Quaid looked at his mother.

"Mother," he said. "Demon and Dad are still inside."

Quaid's mother stroked his hair, to reassure the lad.

"Yes, dear, I know." Then, his mother wiped away her tears. Young Quaid was unsure if it was because he was safe or her husband, young Quaid's father, had been lost. Maybe it was both. She hugged him, and held him tight. She cradled his curved contour, as a bear protected her cub. Young Quaid gazed into his Mother's eyes. His father was no more. Young Quaid's soul could not endure the anguish. He held fast to his mother's grasp, dying a little inside.

Quaid's mind now slipped back to the present; the chapel, the chaplain, their colloquy. Quaid smiled politely and said, "Thank you, father."

"I am merely a servant," replied the priest. "I am happy to be of service."

"Our conversation has been most insightful," said Quaid.

"Insight comes from reflection. Reflection comes from obedience. Obedience comes from prayer," said the priest. As he continued, the priest asked, "Jacob, is there a prayer that you are particularly fond of?" There was a slight hesitation as the holy man continued, "Perhaps we could pray together?"

"The twenty-third Psalm was my father's favoite," Quaid replied.

"The twenty-third Psalm, it is," said the priest.

The worshipers both kneeled. Then, in unison they began. "'The Lord is my sheperd, I shall not want. He maketh me to lie down in green pastures. He leadeth me beside the still waters. He restoreth my soul. He leadeth me in the paths of righteousness for his name's sake. Yea, though I walk through the valley of the shadow of death, I will fear no evil, for thou art with me. Thy rod and thy staff they comfort me. Thou preparest a table before me in the presence of mine enemies. Thou anointest my head with oil. My cup runneth over. Surely goodness and mercy shall follow me all the days of my life. And I will dwell in the house of the Lord, forever, '"[17]

After the resonance, Quaid stood up and stretched out his hand. The priest followed suit.

"Jacob," he said, "God has a plan for you," Quaid's eyes acknowledged the priest's words. He continued, "He has a plan for all of us. Sometimes that work is clear as the morning air. Other times it is clouded as the mountain fog. "The priest looked intently at Quaid for a response, then proceeded. "Look for Him in all that you do, Jacob; and when in doubt, pray."

---

17   Holy Bible - Psalms 23

"I will," replied Quaid. "I will father."

With that, Quaid turned and strode for the door. He did not look back. For Quaid knew, that the cross that was now behind him, would always be in front of him.

CHAPTER 5

As the days passed, Quaid contemplated all that he had seen and heard. He knew not what to think of these developments. Quaid was a quiet, unassuming, man; who preferred the monotony of routine. The challenge of change did not sit well with him. These events became a digestive regurgitation of regularity. As Quaid strode down the street, casually; his mind raced as he reviewed each incident. His mind was lively and loud; while outside it was quiet and hot. Too hot for humans to be out and about, Quaid thought. Internally occupied, Quaid rounded the corner of the town's grocer, and stepped into the alley between buildings.

Bang! Quaid received a sharp blow to the back of the head. The pain surged through his skull as he slumped to the ground dazed. The pang propagated from the occiput to the eyes, and as Quaid glanced up he saw what appeared to be four phantom figures framed above him. Stunned, only indistinct shadows drew against the backdrop of the brilliant sun. As he looked up, Quaid tried to shade his eyes so that he could see his attackers.

"Stay down!" a loud voice commanded.

Quaid, still a bit shaky, tried to ascertain their intent. The situation called for action, but what action, Quaid thought. While his mind was reeling, Quaid's ears pricked up. What was that sound? It was a familiar sound. It was a long and vociferous sound. It filled the air around him. Overtime, it grew, intensified, and drew near. That sound was a snarl, Poe's snarl. Again, Poe had appeared to the aid of his master.

"Call him off!" A voice shouted. Now that the odds had changed, Quaid felt the tide turning. Up on one knee, Quaid readied himself. Bang! A shot rang out. A startled Quaid leapt to his feet. Once rightened, Quaid could see Poe lying on his side in the dust. Red warmth poured from his hind quarters. It flowed over his thigh and pooled onto the brown sand. Quaid reached for his sidearm, but before he could draw his weapon, one man stepped forward from the glob of grey, and pointed his pistol at Quaid's chest.

"Don't more, Marshall."

Quaid froze, as the mass of menace moved in. It was like a pride closing in on the kill. Smack! Quaid's jaw absorbed the full force of a blow from the blind side. The strike landed hard, sending Quaid stumbling. Down he went like a lumberjack's fresh cut tree. Quaid tasted the dry dirt on his tongue. Fervent fluid was felt dripping down from the corner of his mouth. Then there was a silence.

"So, this is the son of the great Matthan Quaid," a voice uttered. "I expected more fight out of you, choirboy."

As Quaid angled his head, he saw a small man holding a revolver. He was well dressed. It was more formal than this one western town had known. All of his attire was hues of grey and black with accents of dark and light. A white pressed shirt and black tie sat above a silk vest. Gold buttons garnished the front with flare. Pleated pressed pants stood straight like an actor on the stage. His hair flowed and waved with a thickness of curl; covered by a sawed-off top hat with a wide brim. Deep eyes hid beneath the brows. A well- groomed mustache filled the center of his face. A scowl screamed down at Quaid. Quaid shouted back, "If you are looking for a fight, a fight you will get. And for harming my wolf, mister, I will see that you are punished."

The stranger grinned. "That was merely a warning shot, choirboy," he said.

Quaid blasted back, "What do you want?" With that, Quaid rose to his feet to face his foe, and queried, "Where are you from?"

"Oh, 'I am from going to and fro on the earth, and from walking back and forth on it,'[18] And as for what I want, choirboy," the gunman paused, then moved in closer, "I want your father."

Before the bandit could elaborate further Quaid blurted out, "My father has been dead for years." Quaid now used this moment to size up his enemies. There were four grey gunmen. The leader was front and center. Shorter that the others he was, but his command presence was palpable. The remaining three fanned out around him like the wings of a bat. They stood taller, wider, and darker with their backs against the bright shining sun. This created a specter of shade which seemed to grow

---

18   Holy Bible - Job 1:7

and start to envelope Quaid, like a serpentine gullet swallows its prey. Each individual had his weapon trained on Quaid. Three had handguns and one a rifle. Quaid glanced over at Poe, motionless. He realized these marauders had no qualms about killing. The loss of life was commonplace in this circle, he thought.

"You are wrong, choirboy!" the leader shouted. "He has been hounding me and my cause for too long. So now, that I know his name," the leader then looked directly at Quaid, "and his progeny, I will bring this war to him."

"And who may I ask are you?" asked Quaid.

"I am Marcus Brutus," he said. The attacker leaned his body toward Quaid, so that his ears could hear him whisper. "Now, where is dear old Dad?"

As the soft speak spun over the leader's lips, Quaid received a blow with the butt of a rifle firmly in the rectus. A ray like pattern of pain spread across his abdomen. The strike knocked out the air from Quaid's lungs as he dropped down to one knee. Quaid gritted his teeth through the hurt. He wanted to go full out into battle, but before Quaid could elicit a response, a second grey figure's fist collided with his chin. Quaid was laid out, flat. Again the gunslinger bent down close to Quaid and exclaimed, "Where is he?"

Blood was now dripping from Quaid's nose. The side of his face was reddened and stung like a wasp's prick. Instinctively Quaid placed his hand on his throbbing jaw, no relief came. Quaid then dragged his hand across his mouth, wiping the dripping red liquid from his lips. The pain clouded his resolve. He thought of his fellow companion's condition. Quaid made an attempt to crawl towards Poe. Again another strike! The toe of a boot struck his chest, sending a sensation of searing suffering throughout his body. The impact flung him over onto his back, gasping for air. Quaid lay lifeless, like a turned turtle; vulnerable.

The small gunslinger stepped forward. With his black boot, he stepped down hard on Quaid's hand. The heel crushed each metacarpal under the pressure. Quaid let out an anguished cry. Unable to move or reach for his weapon, agony overcame him.

"Now that the steak has been softened, it is time for it to be served," said the leader.

Quaid could only watch as the well -dressed gentleman drew his revolver close to his face and pulled back the hammer.

"Well, choirboy, I am waiting," he said. "Where is the man they call the Black Death?"

Quaid had been confused by the beating but even more by the gunslinger's last statement. His attacker continued, "The killer of women and children, the scourge of all humanity; tell me, where is your father?"

Quaid still stunned shook his head slowly back and forth. With all his extremities hurting, and little breath to spare, Quaid was only able to muster enough strength to reply, "My father is dead."

The gunslinger took a step back and dropped his revolver to his side. He looked away from Quaid, expressionless. "I am sorry to hear that choirboy... very sorry. Please then, when you do see him; tell him, I am coming for him." With that the gunslinger began to walk away. As he did, he signaled to his comrades to finish the job.

Quaid felt multiple blows from gun butts and boots. They landed on his already battered body. Quaid's mind started to slip away in all the pain. His last solace was his faith. Quaid began to pray, silently, 'Our Father who art in heaven, hallowed be thy name. Thy kingdom come, Thy will be done, on earth as it is I heaven. Give us this day our daily bread, and forgive us our trespasses. As we forgive those who trespass against us. Lead us not into temptation, but deliver us from evil...' [19]

As the words flashed across his mind, Quaid heard a strange sound. It was a loud clap, like a lightning strike; yet no cloud shone in the bright sky. This was followed by an equally thunderous, click clack. This second sound was more familiar. It was the backward movement that locks the hammer of a double barreled shotgun. Looking around, all Quaid could see was a blinding white light. Quaid attempted to squint as he directed his vision toward the echoed sounds. As Quaid's dazed perception began to reduce, an apparition appeared. Quaid saw what looked like a great elephant with expanding wings. The huge ivory tusks were magnificent. The red glare streaming from the eyes was intense. The rest of the face gave the impression of a fierce lion, with the nose of an eagle. This was a curious sight. Curious, but to Quaid, somehow comforting.

A voice sounded from the dazzling light like a flare, "Hold!"

The blows to Quaid's body suddenly stopped. Quaid blinked, and tried again to glance up. This time, in the middle of the emanating white light was the large figure of a man of color. He was broad as he was tall. His hat was towering and ten gallon.

---

19   Holy Bible - Matthew 6:9

His coat was dusty. His pants were tattered and torn. His boots were weathered and worn. He stood steady. At the ready, he held firmly, both barrels of the long firearm, in his hands.

"I come with power," he said.

The gang in grey stopped the attack. Still, they stood staring, deep into this face, full of darkness. The mountain of a man spoke again, "It would be best to move on." The men in grey quickly comprehended his intensions. The immobilized hostile hitmen tipped their hats reluctantly, then moved off. Quaid turned toward the tower of a black man who had come to his aid and said, "Thank you."

Quaid started to stand, pulling himself up a limb at a time. Quaid dusted the terra from his tattered clothes. Grimacing and still in pain, Quaid fixed his stare over at the giant of a man and managed a smile. Quaid recalled in his head, as he regarded him, 'I have set watchmen upon thy walls, which shall never hold their peace day nor night."[20] As Quaid pondered, the large man spoke, "Your father sent me," he said. Turning and facing his new friend, Quaid's brow raised. "My father?" Quaid questioned.

"My name is Gabriel," he responded. Speechless, Quaid staggered a bit. His quivering quadriceps remained unstable underneath the beaten frame.

Gabriel continued, "I have known your father as long as I am able to remember."

Strange, Quaid thought. "How do you know him?" asked Quaid.

"How does anyone know him?" replied Gabriel.

---

20   Holy Bible - Isaiah 62:6

"Was it from the war?" Quaid asked.

"There have been many wars," said Gabriel.

Quaid, seeing that he was not getting the answers he was seeking, changed his approach. "Well, I am extremely grateful."

"Gratitude is the cornerstone of love," replied Gabriel.

Quaid continued, "You have an artful way of envisioning life."

As quickly as Quaid finished this statement, Gabriel turned and walked toward the sun. It was now glowing orange, and at ground level. The rays painted the desert soil. The surrounding mountains gave off a luminous purple hue. As Quaid watched the movement of the massive figure, it appeared as if the oncoming darkness enveloped Gabriel's body, swallowing it whole. Quaid blinked twice, in an attempt to adjust his sight. All that remained were the lines of shining light projected around his physique. With one more blink, Gabriel and the light were gone.

CHAPTER 6

The day had worn long. Quaid turned his attention back to his injured friend, lying lifeless on the dirt. Quaid bent down and picked up Poe as if he were a newborn. Cradling him tight against his chest, Quaid hastily made his way toward the doctor's office. Quaid could feel the warmth of Poe's body next to his. The fur was soft like a pillow. The contact allowed Quaid to perceive Poe's slowly beating heart. The rythmic throb of life reassured Quaid of Poe's vital condition. A burning flared in Quaid's gut. It was not from the pounding he just took, but from the thought of losing a friend. As his glowing green eyes formed a tear, Quaid gritted his teeth in determination. The sensation of loss spread through Quaid like a virus. He could feel his confidence slipping away like sand in an hourglass. Quaid turned to God, and asked that He not separate him from Poe. As he ran, Quaid pleaded for Poe's life. He hoped that the Almighty could grant the request of a humble servant. Quaid called upon his recollection of First Peter, 'the God of all grace, who hath called us unto his eternal glory by Jesus Christ, after that ye have suffered a while, make you perfect, stablish, strengthen, settle you.'[21]

Quaid reached the doctor's quarters. He rapidly struck the front door with his foot to announce himself. Quaid could see the faint flicker of light from inside, sifting out through the panes of glass in front. "Doc!" Quaid exclaimed, at the top of his voice. He continued banging away, so loud it could have awakened the dead. The door came ajar. Standing there in a white shirt, black pants and suspenders was the town's physician. He was small, had plain features, and dark hair. The doctor was an older man, twice Quaid's age, but his face hid the years well. Quaid peered deep into the dark brown eyes of the surgeon. The murky pools picked up on the Marshall's apprehension.

"Can I help you, Marshall?" he asked.

"Poe has been shot!" said Quaid. "He needs medical attention."

Quaid quickly stepped through the threshold into the main office. There was an examination table positioned slightly off the center of the room, close to the fireplace. Thick wooden cabinets lined the wall. Lead handles adorned each drawer. On the countertop were metal instruments spewed about in a chaotic order. Quaid could see knives, needles, probes, saws, and clamps of ranging shapes and sizes. They were the tools of the trade. Viewing the equipment made Quaid's nerves give his muscles a twitch. The candlelight reflected off all the metal like the twinkling of the stars. The armory of mechanical medical machinery was merely the first layer. Multiple strata of jars were

---

21   Holy Bible - I Peter 5:10

stacked behind the utiliarian utensils. Each appeared to hold specimens of differing variety. There was a heart, a tongue, a pair of eyes. A kidney and liver were represented, even a fully formed fetus. It was eerie. Anatomic study, however, has always been the base of the medical sciences.

Quaid placed the limp form of his friend on the table close to the burning fire. Hanging above the flames was a cauldron, boiling. From the black pot, steam rose from the water as bubbles burst on the surface of the fervid liquid. The scene was almost medieval.

"Ok, Marshall, but I am more of a people person," the doctor said in jest.

"Yes, I know Doc," replied Quaid, slightly irritated by the doctor's half-hearted attempt at humor.

Quaid continued sternly, "Here is a patient that needs care, please tend to him."

The doctor seeing the distress on Quaid's face grabbed his glasses. He slid them over his ears and glanced down at Poe. "Yes, you are right, Marshall," he said. The doctor reached over to the counter and took up his stethoscope. The healer placed it in both ears and gave a listen to Poe's heart and lungs. "Good breath sounds," he said. The doctor then placed two fingers across the wolf's neck, and reported, "Pulse is fine." The doctor turned and walked to the opposite end of his patient. "Let's take a look at this wound," he said.

With Poe lying on his side, both the doctor and Quaid could see the small open hole on the left leg. Fresh blood was still spilling out onto his fur. As the doctor glanced down, it was obvious that no major organs had been injured. The bleeding continued, and the doctor needed to evaluate the vascular system. He took out a hook and a long probe. The doctor pulled back the edge of the wound, it was charred and jagged. He inserted the probe gently and said, "This is going to hurt."

Quaid held Poe steady, placing the balance of his weight against his friend. Poe was weakened, because no struggle was given. The doctor drew back the probe, and confirmed his original observation, "No major artery involved," he said. The doctor stood erect, turned and addressed Quaid, "I believe this patient will make a full recovery."

With a sigh, Quaid said, "Great Doc, but what about the bullet?"

"Bullet?" questioned the doctor. "That little meaningless piece of metal is of no concern. What is worrisome is the loss of blood." The doctor walked briskly over to the raging fire. He placed a thick glove over one hand. The doctor withdrew a long metal rod with a needle pointed tip from the boiling water, like King Arther pulling Excalibur from the stone. He wielded it with an artistry which his years of training had instilled in him. As the doctor placed the pinpoint end at the origin of the bleeding, steam heat rose. The burnt stench reached their nostrils, as the wolf howled. Success. The hemorrhage had been controlled. All that was left was the congealed remains of the once torn dermis.

"Good," said the doctor. "Now, I will apply a little alcohol to keep the wound clean from infection." The doctor shuffled over to the upper cabinet. He reached up and pulled open the double doors to reveal a number of bottles of whiskey, scotch, and wine. The doctor turned his head and glanced back at Quaid. Quaid's eyes were dilated. "It is cheaper to procure in this form," said the doctor in response to Quaid's expression. The doctor selected a bottle of his finest whiskey. He twisted the top, then poured the contents over the leg. The wolf howled again. "There," he said, "now I can dress it."

"Good," said Quaid taking his large frame from on top of the wolf. "I will check on his progress in the morning."

Looking at Quaids battered, and bruised body, the doctor addressed Quaid, "Go home, and get some rest, Marshall. You will both need it to recover."

Quaid thanked the physician, who was already hard at work dressing the wound. Quaid stepped back out through the door and onto the wooden porch. Quaid straightened his bent body. His joints cracked as he adjusted his form. Once fully erect, Quaid made for the jailhouse.

Outside, Quaid beheld his beloved horse, Angel. Still reined, she waited patiently as Quaid approached. A warm feeling spread over Quaid upon seeing his faithful mare. To Quaid what made Angel special was her heart. She knew and loved Quaid like a mother, her child. They had grown together, loved, and lost together. She had carried Quaid in good times and bad. Across lush plains, through dense brush, under the haze of the new moon, she and Quaid had ridden. There was no place on God's good earth she would not go with him. Quaid trusted her, relied on her, and cared for her. He wondered what life would be like without his steed. It would be as a seed drifting in the wind. Their bond was strong. It had been forged from fire.

As Quaid arrived at the front step of the jailhouse, he realized the door had been breached. Quaid withdrew his gun from his holster. He proceeded forth slowly, ready for a fight. As Quaid cautiously moved forward, he could see it was in a state of disarray. His ears became heightened. No sounds emanated from within. All was quiet. Almost too quiet, Quaid thought. Quaid glanced around the corner from the anteroom into the cells in back. No one was home. Apparently, the Friends of the South had been there. For now, Quaid's prisoner had become an escapee.

Quaid holstered his gun, turned, and regarded the mess. What a mess it was; broken furniture, papers and waste spewed across the floor, his desk overturned. Quaid decided it would be best to tackle this in the morning. Besides, he was still stinging from his encounter with the gang in grey. Not to mention, Quaid was hungry and thirsty. Quaid walked out of the jailhouse, and closed the door leaving the destruction behind him. He stepped down and mounted Angel, and said, "Let's go home girl." Off they went quickly, leaving only a dusty trail in their wake. The one western town was silent. As night fell over the surrounding buildings, a blanket of fog rolled in and covered the sleepy village.

Quaid and Angel approached his ranch house. It was dark. The falling sun bathed the mountains in the distance. The reflection shimmered, like reflecting glass. There were deep purples and maroons. The moon could now be seen climbing in the dank dusk. The scene was majestic. Quaid dismounted from Angel and tied her to the front rail post. Quaid was tired, and sore. His stomach was empty and his lips were dry. All he wanted to do was to sit down and have a cup of hot coffee.

Quaid walked across the porch to the front door. He noticed a small beam of light peeking through the frame. Quaid stopped dead. He listened. He heard nothing except the faint crackling of a roaring fire. Quaid calmly took out his gun. This turn of events was not totally unexpected knowing what had recently proceeded, Quaid thought. The door was loosed; so Quaid gently pushed open the wooden barrier with the tip of his gun barrel.

Quaid gazed into the darkness of the den. To his amazement, he could see a shadowy figure sitting in front of the fireplace, with his back towards him. Quaid drew the hammer of his revolver back with a click, just to let the intruder know that he had the drop on him. The figure held fast. Quaid began to recognize the outline. Yes, it was the same contour that Quaid had seen earlier. It was the stranger in grey from the saloon today, Mr. Black.

Quaid spoke first, "Raise your hands where I can see them stranger; or I will send you straight to hell."

A long pause fell upon them. Finally, the stranger replied, "Is it not written, 'Blessed is he who comes in the name of the Lord?'"

"How is it that the Lord sent you?" asked Quaid.

"I have come in the name of the Father," said the stranger. And with that, he slowly stood up and turned to face Quaid. For the first time Quaid could see the full features hidden under that obscuring crown and brim. He was stunned! It was Matthan Quaid, his father.

"What deception is this?" asked Quaid.

"It is the truth, Jacob," said Black.

"The truth I know died years ago in a barn fire," replied Quaid angrily.

"If you do not believe, look outside", Black responded calmly.

Quaid turned his head in the direction of the open front door. There next to his beloved Angel stood her brother, Demon. It was his father's old black Morgan horse. Demon was big, bigger than most Morgans. He was seventeen hands high, and powerful. He appeared dark and ominous, much like the appearance of Black. Demon's ears were pointed and wide-set apart. His head tapered from jaw to muzzle. The muzzle had small firm lips and large wide nostrils. In times of strife, one could imagine fire flaming forth from them. Demon was strength and courage, yet, an extremely well-balanced horse.

"Demon?" Quaid asked Black.

"Why yes," replied Black.

"But it cannot be. I saw you go into the fire, and only Angel came out," said Quaid. He looked up toward Black in a daze. Quaid continued, "For the love of God, Dad, why did you do this thing? I was only a boy! I looked deep into the fury of that fire, and could not go in. I still dream of that night; of you and Demon dying."

Quaid moved over to the chair opposite his father and sat down. A glaze formed across his face. Black sat down in succession, in full view of his son. Quaid quietly continued, "I remember crying all night, me and mother. The next morning when I went out, all was ash."

Black, taken aback by the outpouring of emotion, remained lifeless. Quaid was silent for a time, then he questioned, "So, why all the mystery, father?"

Quaid paused. "Why do you use the name Black?"

Black removed his hat and set it on his knee. He looked directly at Quaid. "In the beginning, I was assigned to a specialized fighting force in the Union army. There was myself and three others. Each had our own unique talent. The government called us the 'point four.' This was in reference to the fact that we were the first in the lines of selected battlefield fronts. As individuals, we were asked to engage in warfare that a standing army could not. We were to no longer refer to our God given names. Each soldier was given a designation, by color. The others were Red, White, and Blue. I was called Black.

Red was a cavalry man, with General Philip Sheridan. He was an expert horseman. Tough and gritty, Red was assigned to General Sheridan by the General-in-chief of the Union Armies. Red led the campaign to Virginia's Shenandoah valley in '64. To the confederates it was an important transportation route and a major source of food. Red lived up to his name by spearheading the mission that turned the valley into a barren waste. It was not just the bloodshed but the fire. Some of the locals called it "The Burning." He later pursued Lee, taking his cavalry deep into rebel strongholds.

White was an infantry man. He took the lead on all major military operations after Vicksburg. White was to infiltrate the Army of Northern Virginia. He was to cause chaos. White broke up chain of command, falsified orders, and created an air of distrust in the fighting units. White was a deceptive master, unafraid to go where only angels dare. His communication expertise kept the Union fully omniscient.

Blue, served with Flagg Officer David Farragut. His duty took him to the seas and waterways. A fantastic sailor and superb swimmer, Blue's abilities were used to trap blockade runners, and help secure positions of naval channels and ports. Blue's base was the USS Hartford, and he played an integral part in the Battle of Mobile Bay. Blue even developed technologies to combat torpedoes and ironclads."

"Do you mean uncle Blue?" asked Quaid.

"Yes, I called him that for your benefit," said Black.

"Uncle Blue taught me to swim," said Quaid.

"You learned from the best, son," said Black.

Quaid began to question his whole life. Maybe it was just a dream, he thought. Quaid searched his mind, who was he really? As Quaid reflected, Black continued.

"These were the colors of the flag. Each man was a prong in a new form of attack. I was called Black. I will spare you the reasoning. Suffice it to say, I was to bring darkness to the light. I went out before General Sherman to carve a path."

Quaid looked over at Black, perplexed.

Black continued, "I was to disrupt patterns of force. I was instructed to breakdown local trust and sever ties to supply chains. I was to make the support and comfort of home not so supportive, or comfortable. It was my job to create havoc, instill doubt in the general public, and bring home the horrors of war.

I travelled in solitude. My job brought me many lonely hours. I did the work not just for my country, but for God. He had called upon me to right this terrible wrong, in which man had enslaved man. When my tour was completed, I returned home to you and your mother. I reared you with the intension of placing this calling in the past. One day, I received a message warning me about a southern fraction that was systematically eliminating the point four, and their families. It was with much trepidation, I staged my own death. In that way, you would be out of danger. It was for you and your mother's protection. Sam gave me his full support. Now, I could pursue and shut down this insurrection unabated. You see Jacob, I am in His service. That is why I am here. I have been tracking the southern assassins. The leader of this rebellion has now come to this one western town. Therefore, I can only assume he knows who you are, Jacob."

Quaid leaned back in his chair. "I have met your assassin, and he claims to be tracking you," said Quaid. "He called himself Marcus Brutus."

Under his breath, Black whispered, "Booth."

Listening attentively, Quaid questioned, "As in John Wilkles Booth?"

"Yes," said Black. "Do you recall your Shakespeare?"

"Yes," replied Quaid. "Marcus Brutus, was Caesar's assailant." Quaid quietly contemplated the implications. "This cannot be," said Quaid.

"Is that so?" retorted Black. "Did you see the picture of him lying dead in the newspaper?"

"I think so," replied Quaid.

"Think again, son," said Black. "If you can recall it was an artist's rendering that depicted his demise. It was not a photograph." Black paused to let what he just said sink in. "Why had Gardner, who had taken all the earth shattering stills of the war, not shot one of Booth's corpse? Why was the family not allowed to see the body?" queried Black. Black looked Quaid straight in the eye. His brow was stern, unmoving. "Jacob, Booth cleverly set that barn on fire as a diversion. When a stray Union soldier came close, he shot him at close range in the head and neck. The burnt, bloodied, disfigured face helped conceal his identity. He merely changed clothing with the dying man during the flaming confusion. Every blueboy was so jubilant about their success; it was days before anyone in the know closely examined the body. By then, Booth had fled, and no photo could be taken for the newspapers."

"By the heavens!" exclaimed Quaid.

"No, by hell itself," said Black. Black began to elaborate. "Booth began a campaign of terror and revenge. Since the war had ended, intelligence concerning the point four leaked out. Booth being a man full of hate began hunting down each member. That is why I had to leave you, Jacob. I used the barn fire to cover my tracks. Kind of apropos, isn't it?" Black continued without hesitation. "I am truly sorry for deceiving you. But I felt it was necessary to preserve the only two things that matter to me here on earth."

Quaid glanced down, pondering all the lost years. At this moment he should be celebrating, but Quaid felt empty inside. He looked back up, and said, "My Pappy was buried years ago. Yet the father I love still lives here in my heart."

Black stood up. He touched Quaid's shoulder with his hand, as in a blessing. "'Thou art my beloved son, in whom I am well pleased,'"[22] he said. With that, Black headed for the door. His outline faded against the night air. Quaid looked up squint-eyed,

---

22   Holy Bible - Mark 1:11

as the dark mirage melted away. Quaid leaped up from his seat in an effort to follow. Upon reaching the entrance, nothing was to be found. There was no Demon, no father, no sound.

CHAPTER 7

Quaid awoke the next morning early. He brushed the sun out of his eyes. Throwing back the blankets, Quaid sat up and placed both feet onto the cold floor. He bent over and placed his face into his hands. He had continued to sleep poorly. Fatigue was a familiar friend. Quaid pushed back his unkempt hair with his right hand. Nothing could fix the damage of the night's work on his mangy mane, but it was worth a try. Quaid's movements, at this hour of the day, were mostly reflex. Quaid stood and walked across the bedroom to his dressing chair. Quaid pulled on his pants and headed for the kitchen. Quaid grabbed a pot and made ready his morning coffee. He lit the stove and placed the pot on top. While the water was reaching a boil, Quaid searched for a clean cup in the pile of dishes in the sink.

Quaid sat at the table where some bread and cheese left over from last night's supper still lay on his plate. He nibbled a bit.

Quaid then walked back to his bedroom. In the corner, opposite his bed was a small wooden cabinet, only three feet high. On it was a cross, and an old tattered Bible. Quaid kneeled down in front of the cross. He picked up the Bible and opened it. He read.

"'Keep yourselves in the love of God, looking for the mercy of our Lord Jesus Christ unto eternal life. And of some have compassion, making a difference. And others save with fear, pulling them out of the fire; hating even the garment spotted by the flesh. Now unto him that is able to keep you from falling, and to present you faultless before the presence of his glory with exceeding joy. To the only wise God our Saviour, be glory, and majesty, dominion and power, both now and ever. Amen.'"[23]

After making the sign of the cross, Quaid rose, and proceeded to the kitchen to retrieve his hot cup of coffee. He poured and drank. The hot, black, liquid energy coursed through his veins. Invigorated and ready, Quaid finished dressing and made his way to the barn. Angel was waiting. Quaid gave her water and food. A fresh carrot from Quaid's pocket, kept her busy as he readied her saddle. After adjusting the tightness of the saddle strap, Quaid mounted.

Quaid rode out into a beautiful morning. The air was crisp and clear. The heat had yet to force the fauna into concealment. This early morning, Quaid proceeded to the ridge which ran by the old colonel's place.

The Colonel had been in the Army of the Potomac. He had served with distinction. The colonel had been in many battles, and was one of the lucky ones to have survived, and with all

---

23   Holy Bible - Jude 1:21

his limbs intact. After the war, the colonel went west. He took a position with the railroad. The colonel had hoped that a change of scenery would go a long way to help him forget days of anguish, pain, and death.

Now that the colonel and the railway had parted ways, he owned a large spread of land. His ranch was covered in cattle. He raised all form of animal, including chickens, goats, horses, and milk cows. The colonel tended the land as well. Crops did well after the colonel created an irrigation system for his land. The colonel and his wife resided in the main house. They had one child, a daughter, Samantha Katherine. The colonel was a private man, so he had but one ranch hand, John Henry.

John Henry was born a slave. During the war, the colonel discovered John Henry wandering aimlessly through the brush. Even though on patrol, the colonel stopped, fed, and clothed John Henry. 'But a certain Samaritan, as he journeyed, came where he was. When he saw him, he had compassion on him. He went to him, and bound up his wounds, pouring in oil and wine, and set him on his own beast, and brought him to an inn, and took care of him.'[24] When the colonel's regiment came across John Henry in the wood, the colonel could only see a child of God. How could he leave God's own child helpless, hungry, and homeless? The colonel brought John Henry along for the remainder of his tour of duty, as his adjutant.

John Henry had no family. All were killed in the conflict. He was alone. Yet John Henry was a kindhearted man. Physically, John Henry was large; broad in build, strong in stature. One could see the swollen musculature through the burlap coverings

---

24   Holy Bible - Luke 10:33

he used for clothing. His skin was dark. His eyes were bright. John Henry's hair was cut short. It was a tight cropped style. John Henry hardly ever smiled in those days, but when he did, the elation of the expression lit up the whole room. One could not help but be moved to joy as you viewed the child-like visage.

Being an honorable man, John Henry wanted to repay the colonel's kindness. John Henry's heart was as big as his hands and feet. Being grateful, John Henry enlisted, and served as the colonel's aide until the end of the war. Their quest to free the captives was their common goal. After the war, John Henry offered to continue his work for the colonel. He was a loyal friend, someone the colonel could count on at the railroad. Since John Henry had no living relatives, the colonel invited him to join his family. John Henry accepted. Despite being close to the colonel, John Henry worked harder than any other man under the railroad's employ. While the colonel was busy as the railway's brass hat, John Henry became the best gandy dancer on the rail. Every caller wanted John working his line. He could drive spikes faster and more efficiently than any other man. He wielded his hammer as if it were a child's toy. Under his might, it was weightless, effortless. After much profit had been accumulated, the colonel left the railroad, retired, and raised his cattle. John Henry was the colonel's family. So, being a forthright follower, he turned in his hammer to till the land and tend the herds.

John Henry was not educated, but he spoke well. His baritone voice could soothe a snake. Quaid enjoyed his conversations with John Henry. He had a unique view of the world that Quaid appreciated. The diversion of listening to John Henry's life stories empowered Quaid with the full belief in God's sovereignty. Imagining each narrative was serene, surreal, for Quaid. Quaid's favorite tale was of John Henry's name. Being a slave, John Henry had the name of a slave; that of his owner. When he was freed, John Henry never spoke that name again.

"My first and middle name will do just nicely," John Henry said. "A man's name is his foothold in history. It signifies, clarifies, certifies, and justifies a man. All that you are, all that God knows of you, are held in that name. I am he. He is me. I am the name, and the name is me." Quaid understood.

Quaid had been on his way to the jailhouse. Something in Quaid rose up and touched his thoughts. Quaid's intuition was strong. It was a part of his calling. 'But ye are a chosen generation, a royal priesthood, a holy nation. A peculiar people that ye should show forth the praises of him who hath called you out of darkness into his marvelous light.'[25] Overcome by curiosity, Quaid grabbed Angel's reins tight, and turned her down the steep incline. The colonel's ranch house quickly came into focus. A cold sweat broke on Quaid's face as he approached. This was a strange happening on such a hot western day. As he drew near, Quaid expected to see the colonel or Dotty, his wife, working in the yard. There was no appearance from little Samantha running out to greet him. No silence ever spoke so loudly to Quaid. His pulse quickened. His eyes dilated. He took a quick deep breath. Then, Quaid swallowed hard in preparation for the coming confrontation. Angel stopped short. Quaid quickly dismounted and immediately withdrew his pistol. The search was on.

---

25   Holy Bible - I Peter 2:9

Quaid entered the main residence through the front door. The sitting room was in shambles. An obvious struggle had taken place. It was still, no sounds, no signs. Quaid moved with stealth across the floor, tracking. There was no movement. Quaid made his way to the back of the house. He entered the kitchen. It had the appearance of the usual galley. Hanging pots and pans, stacked bowls and dishes filled the room. The fire on the stove was lit and roaring; it gave off waves of warmth. Down on the floor, Quaid saw a pool of red. "By the heavens," Quaid whispered under his breath. His eyes followed the line of the liquid backwards; and there at the end, lay the colonel and Dotty, both lifeless.

Quaid bent down on one knee. He had to check both bodies for any signs of life. Quaid layed his hands on the colonel. There was no rise and fall on the chest. Quaid placed his fingers on the colonel's neck, no pulse. He was still warm to the touch, no rigor. Quaid had to be certain of his diagnosis. He placed his ear down against the colonel's left breast. No sound. No beat. No life. The colonel was gone. The ambient temperature seemed exceedingly higher to Quaid. Sweat started to form on his brow. Quaid moved over to Dorthea. She too, was still. Quaid directed himself to the purpose at hand, and placed his ear against her chest. Quiet. Quaid's lip quivered. He felt a strong emotion well up inside. But at present, Quaid had no time for sympathies. Quaid knew he had to act fast. Two more lives were yet at stake, and they would depend on what he did next. Quaid rose quickly, and with precision, inspected each room. Nowhere was little Samantha to be found.

Quaid ran out the door, and rushed over to the barn. It was an old wooden structure. Well kept, it was painted and pristine. The weather, however, had cut cracks and wrinkles in the facets of its form. Quaid forcefully pushed open the large hinged doors as the light of day poured into the dark interior like a waterfall. There he saw in the middle of the barn, tied up like a rodeo steer, John Henry. He was lying on one side, bound and gagged so that he could not cry out. He was squinting, as one would, to look directly into the sun. He tried to glance up. At least he was alive, Quaid thought. Quaid reached down to undo his bonds, and could not help but think John Henry had been left to die.

Quaid helped John Henry to his knees, he was still somewhat dazed and dehydrated. John Henry grasped Quaid as if to steady himself. Quaid got right to the point and asked,

"What happened?"

"Five men, dressed in grey," said John Henry. "They just appeared on the front porch, looking for the colonel. They kicked in the door, and shot the colonel and Miss Dorthea. I tried to stop 'em Marshall but I had no gun. They tied me up, and took Samantha."

Quaid could hear the distress in John Henry's speech. Quaid knew that John Henry had tried to protect Samantha.

"Which way did they go?" asked Quaid.

"I am not sure," replied John Henry. He hesitated, then began again. "They bound me. One of them said 'Hang 'em.' Another said 'shoot him like a dog.' Then their leader stepped forward. He wore a dark grey hat. He had black hair and a full mustache. His cold eyes peered down at me as if he was looking into the Abyss. Then he said, 'No. I will not waste bullets on the likes of him. Let him rot.' They hoisted Samantha onto one of their horses and took off."

Quaid asked, "How long ago?"

"Not long," John Henry replied.

Quaid stood up, "Can you ride?" Quaid asked.

"Yes," said John Henry.

Quaid whistled loudly for Angel. She came running, as if lightening had struck. Quaid shouted at John Henry, "Go for your horse!"

John Henry mounted a tall brown and white Mustang. It was a mixed beast that he had captured from the plains. Once wild, now a well trained filly. She responded with a shake of the head. Out of the barn they galloped. As they rode forward, Quaid and John Henry heard gunshots ring out in the distance. Quaid's face went pale. He glanced over at John Henry. His was the look of panic. Both men knew that time had run out.

The horses made like a river's rapids running downstream. As they rounded the top of the hilly pasture, a pounding thunder filled their ears. It was an increasing resounding storm that both men had become familiar with. It was that distinctive, that repetitive, that destructive discharge. The two men looked out over the valley, and the full strokes of the artists brush came into view. The picture was a portrait of power, moving in mass toward a small singularity. Quaid sat up high in his saddle. He gazed over the landscape which was now flowing like a tidal wave toward a little girl. She had been bound and left to be trampled by a streaming stampede.

Quaid quickly formed a plan. He turned to John Henry and shouted, "I will head off the lead. You swing around ahead, and on a diagonal, and go for the girl."

Without a further word, their steeds took to the task, with a burst; hurling them toward the massive, moving, mountain of mammoths.

Quaid pursued a parallel course in an attempt to cut off the pack. Quaid could feel his heart race, almost at the pace of his horse. Quaid rode as never before, focused and without fear. Quaid thought; Lord, now is the time for a miracle, not for Quaid's sake, but for this young girl. Quaid encouraged Angel to pick up the pace. The rushing wind coursed across his lips, drowning Quaid's vibrating vocal cords. No natural force could contain the words of Quaid's prayer to our redeemer as he rode. "'Soul of Christ, sanctify me. Body of Christ, save me. Blood of Christ, inebriate me. Water from the side of Christ, wash me. Passion of Christ, strengthen me!'"[26]

John Henry rode off in an angled path. He aimed at an attempt to rescue. John Henry realized the danger, but this was for a child, for his family's child, for his child. His anger grew,as John Henry pressed forward. The fury turned to gritty determination; he pushed his horse ever harder and faster.

Quaid could now see the lead bull. He checked his arsenal. No bullets, thought Quaid; gunfire may only add to the confusion and rampage. He would employ the rope. As Quaid drew closer to his target, he began swinging his lariat above his head. His hat flickered in the sun as the rope swung around eclipsing the white waves of light. More and more Quaid drew

---

26   Catholic Prayer - Prayer to our Redeemer

into the herd. Screaming and kicking until there was no more to draw out of his ride, Quaid pressed in farther. Quaid ran Angel right up into the rush. Quaid could hear his horse's legs roaring synonymously with the bulls. The sound was so loud; Quaid could not hear himself think. The wind blew hard as he drew his hand to release the noose. A large gust exploded into him, lifting Quaid across the herd in proximity to the lead. The blast told Quaid the time was now. Quaid let the lariat fly, entangling the raging bull, bringing him down. A cascade of tumbling torrents followed. Dust flew. The haze clouded the sun, as the horde swarmed around the fallen like bees to the hive. Quaid could see he split the stampeding surf. His heroics had not yet ended the peril. It was John Henry's turn.

John Henry approached the little lady like a hawk making a run at its prey. As John Henry drew closer; out of his peripheral field of view, he saw what appeared to be an enlarging dark shadow. It came out of the east. It grew larger as John Henry drew closer, and closer. It's hue was black. Black on black. It was a man. It was a man on a horse. He seemed to be riding almost on air.

John Henry heard a loud eruption, like a hammer striking an anvil; breaking open a seal. John Henry thought he heard a voice whisper, "Come and see." And lo, John Henry could easily visualize a dark horse gliding over the plain flowing in unison with an even darker figure atop. The horseman wielded a metal instrument in his hand, but John Henry could not make it out. John Henry kicked his horse into high gear. He could feel the mounting pressure from the west, that of the approaching beasts.

In the east, the shadow of a man came on like an avenging angel. John Henry's head was reeling. His ominous task now became officious, by the obvious outline of a rebel outlaw. The shadow reached back with one arm and withdrew a battle axe from a hidden holster strapped behind his back. The blade was broad, keen, and curved. It was engraved with markings that appeared to undulate. Strapped to a thick stick, the sharp steel glared in John Henry's vision. As he looked away, John Henry's eyes met Samantha's. Fear turned to hope. He was almost there. Then, it flew. End over end, over end, the axe went whirling toward John Henry. It travelled in an instant. In that time, John Henry reached his destination. In a Cossacks drag, John Henry rolled left over the side of his horse. His muscular bicep extended down and grasped the fragile figure of the little girl. The axe, flying fast in John Henry's direction; careened closely to his carotid, and passed by, landing and leveling an oncoming bull. The impact forced it down, dropping short of Samantha and her savior. With power, John Henry pulled up Samantha with one motion, onto the safety of his saddle. John Henry sat forward and quickly cut the Mustang, striding past the dark rider. John Henry headed for the clearing, quickly.

Quaid rode up and met John Henry with a smile. His steed stopped short. Angel appeared so majestic, and Quaid upon her, the conquering hero. John Henry held the little girl tightly in his arms. Quaid thought he would never let go. Quaid could see John Henry holding back the tears. Quaid, reassured, let go with a sigh of relief. Just as Quaid felt that serene sensation pass over him, the mood changed. The air became thick, the sky darkened. Quaid heard the hoof steps of an approaching horseman. Quaid glanced over his shoulder. Stunned, he could see it was his father, Matthan Quaid. He came galloping, upon Demon, headed in their direction.

Quaid could see John Henry's altered attitude. John Henry quickly dismounted and took a position of defense. Quaid followed down, but then slowly proceeded forward toward his father. Black pulled back on Demon's reins.

"Hold," Black said softly.

Then he addressed Quaid.

"Son, is everyone safe?"

"Yes," replied Quaid.

Black continued, "I came as soon as I was called."

Quaid looked at him curiously. John Henry backed off as the specter of a man dismounted from his horse. Quaid turned and saw John Henry's reluctance to engage Black. Quaid tried to intervene by reaching out to John Henry but he spun away mumbling.

"What did you say, John Henry?" asked Quaid. John Henry had turned his back upon the phantom before him. His memory lit a fuse of fear. John Henry stuttered, "He is ... he is ... He is the Black Death."

Quaid looked at his father as he never had before. Who was this man? What had he done to illicit such a response? Had the lawman met the face of lawlessness and seen his own reflection? No, Quaid thought, no.

John Henry encircled his arms around Samantha, as he tried to gather his facilities. He then repeated his statement, this time more firm and clear. "Marshall, he is the Black Death, what we called the avenger of blood." John Henry seemed to fall into a trance and in a monotone, he spoke. "'Lest the avenger of blood pursue the slayer, while his heart is hot, and overtake him, because the way is long, and slay him.'"[27]

Quaid turned to his father and asked, "What does he mean?"

No response was given. With more force, Quaid asked, "Are you called the Black Death?"

Black replied, "I have been called many names."

Quaid sternly asked again, "Are you of whom he speaks?"

"Yes," said Black.

Quaid looked over to John Henry for answers. John Henry bent down and released his little fledgling. John Henry then stood tall. He began to speak slowly. "The Black Death came to the South during the war for freedom. He hit like a plague. He killed thousands; men, women, and children. Word of his destruction spread throughout the South. Many believed that he was God's own avenger of blood from the Old Testament. He would be sent to take the lives of those who took life. This time, though, there would be no cities of refuge. The destroyer laid waste, cleansing with fire, and leveling all in his path. Few have seen him and lived to speak of it." John Henry paused. He peered over at Black.

John Henry's memory had been mired by all the years. After a few moments, the past came into focus once more. He continued "They were going to hang ... hang us all."

"Who?" asked Quaid.

"The rebels," said John Henry.

---

27   Holy Bible - Deuteronomy 19:6

"The confederates came and pulled my family out of our beds. I can still see the flickering fire of the torches leading us out to the trees. They beat the men, whipped the women. Our home was set on fire. As it raged, preparations were made for a mass hanging. Amiss all the turmoil, I heard a rebel cry out. One by one, each man in grey fell. All were dead. It was the Black Death. He blew in like a whirlwind and slew unseen. Soon, every soldier lay lifeless. I glanced up from my bondage and I saw his rage. He looked down at me and said, 'You are free.' Then without a whisper, he was gone."

Just as John Henry delivered those words, Quaid had turned to see that his father was no longer there. Quaid's attention turned back to John Henry and Samantha. The little girl was still in shock, and clinging tightly to John Henry's hand. Her delicate little fingers looked like porcelain buried in his paw. She looked up at Quaid. With streaks of washed away dirt on her face from the stream of tears that had once flowed, she smiled. John Henry looked down at his precious brown-haired doll. His heart was filled with sadness over the realization that she was now an orphan. Yet, John Henry beamed with the fullness of joy to see her standing next to him, free from harm.

Quaid broke the ice. "John Henry," he said. "I do charge you into service as a deputy, for the United States of America."

John Henry replied, "I am ready."

Quaid continued, "John Henry, I order you to go home."

"What?" said John Henry.

"I want you to ensure Samantha's safety."

"Are we not going after the killers?"

"Not just yet," said Quaid. "You must attend to more important matters. You are all the family she has left, John," said Quaid. He placed his hand on John Henry's shoulder. John Henry knew what had just been entrusted to him. He was now to be a parent. He softly smiled, and said, "Yes, Marshall." He nodded in acceptance. "She is my family. I will give her all the love she needs." John Henry hesitated. As he contemplated all the years gone by, all the tragedy; was he now prepared to be happy?

"I may be no father," said John Henry, "but I am able to become one."

Quaid grinned. "Thank you," he said. "You are about to undertake the toughest job on God's earth. I will send you my prayers."

With that, Quaid climbed aboard Angel. He pointed her towards town. Riding off, Quaid turned and tipped his hat. It was a job well done.

CHAPTER 8

After a full afternoon of pencil pushing at the jailhouse, Quaid was ready to call it a day. All the excitement from the morning had made his usual filing of forms seem almost welcomed. Quaid placed the final period on the page, then pushed back from his seat at his desk. He turned and grabbed his hat off the hook, placed it on his head, then proceeded out the front door. It was getting dark. Angel stood at the ready. She barely shone in the dusky light. Without a word, Quaid climbed on, and headed for home.

Quaid pulled back on Angels reins as he came upon his front porch yet again. It seemed to Quaid that every time he returned home, fatigue had been his companion on the journey. Dusty and tired Quaid swung himself from his mount to the ground. Quaid pulled up the belt on his loose pants, straightened his posture, and made for the door. Quaid knew that serenity lie on the other side of that door. That, and a cold drink of water.

Quaid pushed through the wooden passage and strode into the front sitting room. Quaid lit the fire. He stepped briefly into the kitchen. He grasped the cool drink of well water he had been longing for all day. Quaid removed his hat, and poured some of the liquid refreshment over his head. Quaid felt his spirit rejuvenated like a baptism. The cold sensation spread across his form, dropping down onto his shoulders and sinking into his soul. It brought a moment of joy in an otherwise troublesome day. Moving back into the front room, Quaid looked for a good resting place. He let out a sigh as he laid his large frame into the rocking chair. The fire was warm. It felt like a soft wool blanket had been draped over him. He was home.

Quaid glanced over at the table and lamp, next to his chair. He reached over, and grabbed the lamp, Quaid stood. He walked over to the flowing fire and lit the lamp. He placed it gently back on the table. There, under the light of the lamp, was an old black and white photo from his youth. It was one of the few pictures Quaid had of his family.

As Quaid sat back in his chair, he continued to look at the photo. It was Angel and Demon, standing chest to chest. Quaid was on one side, his father was on the other. They were both holding their reins. In the picture, the youthful Quaid was smiling. His white teeth shone. The corners of his mouth reached up into his cheeks and forced his eyes to squint down into thin isles of emotion. Quaid could still feel the joy that precipitated. A child's expression of pleasure had exploded from under his hat. The hat which was two sizes too big. Quaid had looked at the photo a thousand times yet on this occasion he saw something new. Quaid's father had the same smile. His face was stone solid, without a wrinkle; ageless. The light seemed to reflect from its surface like a crystal. The transfixed jubilance seemed to brighten the longer Quaid looked. His father was happy. He was proud. His father showed an emotion only seen in the company of his son. As Quaid inspected the image, he realized that his father, like the old photo, had created an indelible bond between them. It was the love of a father for his son.

Quaid reached over and picked up the picture. He held it tight. Quaid closed his eyes. His memory slipped back to that place and time. It was a time on innocence, when the sounds of the horses, his mother's voice, and the look of his father, brought a sense of security and peace.

Quaid visualized his father kneeling down next to him to talk and give advice.

"Jacob, you are my son, and I will always want to be here with you. But, sometimes, circumstances dictate our actions. Even more important, we must fulfill God's will."

Quaid remembered being fearful of that statement. No boy wants to lose his father. Young Quaid replied, "Pappy I thought you were done fighting the war. I do not want you to leave. Please, Pappy."

Tears started to swell in young Quaid's eyes as he looked directly into his father's weathered brow. Just as Jacob started to sniffle, his father took him in his arms.

"Son, we must all go to God when we are called. Do not be afraid for He is always with you. You must not fear any man, or anything. Place your faith in God. You see, my son, it is from Him that we draw strength."

As Quaid's father spoke, he began to wrap his gigantic bear-like arms tighter around young Quaid.

"Strength?" Jacob inquired.

"Yes," said his father." Real strength lies not in the hands, but in the heart. Remember those words, Jacob, and carry them with you always."

Young Quaid smiled. His father continued. "'Do not fear those who kill the body but cannot kill the soul. Rather fear Him who can destroy both soul and body.'"[28]

"I am not sure I understand, Pappy," replied Jacob.

"Let me simplify it for you, Son," said his father. "Recall your teachings, Jacob. The Bible tells us to fear the Lord; that leads to life. He who knows it rests satisfied. He who knows and understands will not be visited by harm. So, son, fear no man."

"I see, Pappy," Jacob responded.

"Ok, son," his father said, "It has been a long day. Now, go on inside and prepare for bed."

Quaid remembered just how long that day had been. Quaid's mind drifted back to later that night. There was a commotion outside. Young Quaid awoke and sat up in bed. "The horses," he whispered across his lips. Young Quaid ran to the front door and threw it open. He looked out to see the barn engulfed in flames. A tall, dark figure stood out front. Young Quaid recognized the outline of his father. "Pappy!" young Quaid called out.

Quaid closed his eyes tighter. A scowl came across his face. He did not want to travel down the road of despair again. The pain he felt at losing his father. The helplessness of the moment

---

28   Holy Bible - Matthew 10:28

was too much to bear. Quaid forced the memory from his mind. He wanted to push forward to the days that followed, and his need to do God's will. 'Be not conformed to this world, but be ye transformed by the renewing of your mind. That ye may prove what is good, and acceptable, and perfect, the will of God.'[29]

The sun was shining once more. Young Quaid was out in the front forty attending to his chores. The labor helped him to forget the pain of his recent loss. As young Quaid toiled, he noticed a figure in the distance. It approached steadily. It was a man. It was a man on a horse. It was a short man, but he sat tall in the saddle. As he came closer, young Quaid could see a lit cigar. The smoke was streaming from his mouth. He had piercing eyes, which shone through the years of ruggedness that had been built on his countenance. A beard covered his face. His nose was long and somewhat crooked. The man's dress was common, like a farmer's. It was mostly dark blue with gold and brass buttons. The man wore a jacket loosely around his small shoulders. He seemed to wear it like a crown. Young Quaid felt no fear. There was no sense of danger about him.

The man slowed his horse to a walk. Step by step, the stranger came closer. Young Quaid held his ground, but tightened the grip on his pick axe. The man pulled up on his horse. Stopped, he looked down at young Quaid. "Are you Jacob?" He asked.

"Yes, sir," relied young Quaid.

The horseman continued, "I am your uncle, Sam." Young Quaid looked at him curiously. "I have traveled a great distance to see you and your mother. Is she at home?" He questioned.

"Yes," replied young Quaid.

---

29   Holy Bible - Romans 12:2

"Forgive me, Jacob," Sam said. "We have not yet met." He paused. "I was very close to your father. When I heard about the accident, I came immediately to offer my assistance."

Young Quaid looked up not knowing what to say. Finally, young Quaid blurted out, "He is a magnificent horse, sir."

"Thank you, Jacob. Please, call me Sam. Then Sam continued, "His name is Butcher. He is my faithful companion." Sam stretched out his hand in the direction of young Quaid. "May we give you a lift to the house?"

"Yes! Yes!" said young Quaid with glee. Young Quaid clasped Sam's hand and leapt up onto the back of Butcher. Sam took a long draw from his stogie, then said, "Forward, Butcher!"

Young Quaid could feel the power of Butcher's stride as they moved. A small smile snuck out over young Quaid's face for the first time since the accident. The air was crisp. The wind generated by Butcher, blew by his little yellow locks. It gave young Quaid the feeling of flying. Jacob held tightly to Sam as the speed increased.

Young Quaid's uncle did not speak during the entire trip. Young Quaid began to wonder what sort of man his uncle was. Something inside young Quaid spoke to him. It said that this man was more than a beard and smoking cigar. Young Quaid hoped to know more of this man's history, and of his dealings with his father.

Sam pulled up in front of the house. He helped young Quaid back to earth. Sam dismounted as well. After straightening his hat and coat, he looked at young Quaid and said, "Please inform your mother that I am here." Sam waited patiently as young

Quaid bounced through the front door. Excitedly, he rushed into the kitchen and grabbed his mother's apron.

"Mother, uncle Sam is here!"

Slowly, she turned toward her jubilant son. She looked long and lovingly down at him. She replied calmly. "I knew he would come."

Without hesitation, she continued, "Jacob, bring Sam in and let him rest by the fire. He has journeyed far and long." Young Quaid hurried back to Sam's side and said, "Come in uncle."

Sam reached up to his mouth and pulled the burning tobacco from it. Sam had a look of disgust on his brow as he thrust it down to the ground. He crushed it underfoot while under his breath young Quaid heard, "Damn waste." Sam looked up at the lad who was watching his every move.

"Sorry you saw that son," Sam said, "Vices are vile vestments of vexed vanities."

Young Quaid tilted his head, as he attempted to contemplate his uncle's verbiage. Sam could see the perplexed expression on the boy's persona. He stopped and tried another approach. "There is a reason why they call them bad habits, Jacob," said Sam. Young Quaid nodded in the affirmative. Sam took young Quaid's hand in his and they strode forward together. Once inside Sam stood erect, as if at attention. He waited for young Quaid's mother to appear. When she entered, Sam stepped towards her and raised his arms. He hugged her tightly. After the embrace, Sam said, "I am sorry, Bea. You know how much I loved him. Please accept my condolences."

Young Quaid's mother turned her head to hide the tears falling from her angelic face. Before the dam broke, she glanced back at Sam and said, "Sam, you must be hungry after coming all this way. Can I offer you some cucumbers?"

"Of course," Sam replied. "That would be grand, thank you. You know they are my favorite."

"Come and rest by the fire," said Bea.

Sam removed his hat, and reclined back in the rocking chair. Young Quaid sat next to him as his mother returned to the kitchen. Now alone, Sam looked deeply into young Quaid's eyes. He said, "Son, I want to tell you a little bit about your father."

Young Quaid was glued to the spot. His heart skipped a beat. He took a deep breath. Sam continued, "Jacob, your father was the most fearless man I have ever known. He had tremendous strength. Not just physical strength, but an inner strength that only comes from above. He spent his life in servitude. It was in the service that we met. I quickly realized that he was an expert horseman, rifleman, and swordsman. He had abilities no other man had, or imagined. However, it was our very first meeting that will never leave my mind.

Sam pushed back in his chair. Young Quaid could see he was gathering his thoughts, forming a pattern of remembrance. It was like Sam had entered into a trance. He continued. "I was in command. I had come that day to try to give inspiration to the fallen troops. Your father was lying in a field hospital. He had been wounded multiple times, twelve gunshots in all. He had been pushed to the side, given up for dead. No one seemed to notice him there in the corner of the medical tent; unmoving, bloodied, barely breathing. As I drew close, he called out to me. I walked over to him to hear his request. As he lay in torment, he asked if he could pray for me." Sam stopped, still contemplating the magnitude of the moment. Sam continued. "Pray for me? I was a man with no wounds, no pain, no suffering; and he wanted to pray for me. I was so moved by his faith I decided to return the next day. Expecting to see his death, I was amazed when I found your father sitting up in bed, smiling. It was as if he knew I would be coming. He asked if I had come to pray. I said, yes. I came back each day thereafter. We knelt, and thanked God. His perseverance and power were unequalled. I knew this man was special, not because of his physical prowess; it was his faith." Sam paused and he looked deep into Quaid's eyes. "He had a deep faith. 'Seest thou how faith wrought with his works, and by works was faith made perfect.' [30] I see him in your eyes, son."

Young Quaid was moved. A tear ran down one side of his face. Sam stood to comfort him. Young Quaid looked up at his bearded uncle and said, "I was not strong enough."

"What do you mean, Jacob?" Sam asked.

"I was not strong enough to save my father." Young Quaid tried to continue through the tears. As if out of breath, young Quaid stopped. He sobbed, "I was afraid." Sam could see the agony on his face. Through the pain, young Quaid continued. "I was not strong enough to save my father, uncle."

Sam placed his hand on young Quaid's quivering shoulders. His grip was firm but consoling.

"Listen to me, Jacob. Do not blame yourself for something you could not control." Young Quaid had stopped crying long enough to hear Sam's words. Sam continued. "Fear not son, I know that your father was extremely proud of you. He loved you with all his heart. He would not want you to think

---

30   Holy Bible - James 2:22

these thoughts." Sam paused, seeing young Quaid's state had improved. He continued then, to finish his thoughts. "Jacob, a wise man once told me, 'true strength lies not in the hands, but in the heart.' I have carried that truth with me my whole life."

Young Quaid recalled the repetition of his father's own words. He felt his father's love. Young Quaid's mind slowed. The passages went through his mind again as his father had delivered them. 'True strength, Jacob lies not in the hands, but in the heart.' Young Quaid finished the quotation moving his lips with a whisper, "The heart of God." It felt as if his father was still there. Young Quaid could feel his father's warmth, like warmth of a fire.

The heat from the fire broke a sweat on Quaid's face, breaking his concentration. He awoke from the daydream still resting in the rocking chair. His large hands placed the photo back on the table. The memory, he placed back into his intellect. Weary, sleep overcame Quaid, as tranquility filled his heart.

CHAPTER 9

The next morning, Quaid awoke to find himself still in the rocker by the fire. What was once a roaring, red rage; was now only embers. Quaid could feel the stiffness of his joints as he rose from the chair. He stretched to break the tightness he felt in his muscles. Quaid yawned as he heard the growl of his stomach declaring his hunger. Quaid walked slowly towards the kitchen. His gait was rigid and graceless, but he was still able to manage despite this temporary impediment.

Once in the kitchen, Quaid grabbed a handful of coffee beans and a large piece of bread. Quaid reached over to his cup, and took a small sip. Cool to the tongue, Quaid tipped his head back as he drank the remaining fluid. He wanted to get moving. Booth was still on the loose. Quaid decided to eat, as he often did, on the run. Quaid adopted the old Union soldier's habit, and carried some coffee beans in his pocket. As he went, Quaid chewed the bitter brown beans. He delighted in the dose of digitoxin-like alkaloid elixir. His saliva stimulated the liquefaction of flavor. Quaid savored, then, swallowed.

Quaid checked his weapons. The six-shooter was loaded. Extra bullets filled his belt. Rifle was ready. Ammunition was also available in his saddle bag. Bowie knife, throwing knife, pocket dagger, were all sharpened, shining, and secured. His amble arsenal all waited at the ready.

Quaid rode into town on Angel. It was still early morning but the sun was already scalding hot. Sweat appeared on Quaid's brow. Angel strode past the general store to the jailhouse. Quaid stopped, stepped down from Angel, and tied her firmly to the post; where she could have ample shade. Quaid moved across the porch and pushed open the jailhouse door. To Quaid's surprise, there behind his large ornate wooden desk was Black.

"Nice piece of lumber you have here, son," said Black. "I bet it came at no small cost."

Quaid, not in the mood for small talk retorted, "Cost is something the Black Death would know well." Quaid stepped forward, then, continued. "The Black Death was responsible for mass devastation. What was the cost of entire southern cities burning to the ground? What was the cost of the destruction of southern society? Grave mounds were filled with rebel soldiers, murdered women, and children. The bodies were piled so high they could be seen for miles. So, what is the cost of the deaths of those who were innocent?"

Black stood up, visibly disturbed. He replied angrily, "No man is innocent. And, women and children who give aid to an enemy who enslaves are not without the cloud of sin."

Quaid approached Black with even more stern determination on his face. "You cannot justify those actions," said Quaid.

Agitated and unmoved, Black responded. "When war is waged, it must be won. As for you, Jacob, I do not need to justify the callings of God to anyone. When He calls, I come. His people were enslaved. I was to free them."

"Your methods were hardly honorable," replied Quaid. Quaid raised his voice further, "Torture, taking lives at random, turning city squares into rubble, all are real aspiring acts of heroism," said Quaid soundly with sarcasm.

Black moved in close, like he was moving in for a kill. "You were not there. You did not face the mourners, as I. You did not witness the abuse. You did not feel the agony. You have no experience in war. You have no right to use those words!" exclaimed Black.

"I do not have to experience war to know right from wrong. To know, good, from evil," said Quaid.

Black became angry. He stared down Quaid from under his dark hat. His lips were pursed and firm. His eyes ablaze, they burned through Quaid with a fury. Black took a breath, then, replied back more firmly. "Good from evil? How do you begin to tell me of evil? My time here on earth has given me first-hand knowledge of evil." There was a short interruption as Black's blood boiled. He continued. "This 'evil' you speak of could not have brought you into the world. And seeing that I did bring you into this world; I can surely take you out!" As Black finished his sentence, his face was so close to Quaid's, he could see the steam rising from his skin. Black fumed. His scowling nose almost touched Quaid's. The look was serious, as serious as life and death.

Quaid, undaunted, replied, "I fear no man!"

A hint of a smile crept back into Black's countenance. His posture changed. He stepped back. Black nodded, then, began to turn away. As Black turned, he said softly, "No, I believe you do not." Black again turned toward Quaid. "I have taught you well, my son." Black added, "In many ways, your approach to justice has added more strength. You have become more than who I am. You have incorporated the greatest gifts of your mother as well. God bless you."

A soft glow came over Quaid. He recalled his mother's voice, her gentle touch, and the loving way she approached each day. Quaid realized he was the best of both worlds. He was the best part of his father, and the best part of his mother; combined. Quaid smiled with satisfaction.

"Son," Black started back. "I did not come here to do battle with you. Do not worry, my past actions will be judged by one much larger than you. I only came here to ask that you stay away from Booth." Black began to walk away.

"Are you planning to kill him?" Quaid asked. Black stopped. He gave no response. Quaid continued, "You said there will be one larger to judge your actions. Do you plan on being that judge by killing Booth?"

"I am no judge," said Black after pausing. He turned and faced Quaid again. "I am merely going to send Booth to his judgment." With that, Black strode out the front door. Quaid watched as the door closed, almost as if the door between father and son had closed.

Frustrated by the fiery exchange, Quaid walked slowly over to his chair behind the desk, and sat down. His mind was reeling. What was he to do? Was he to listen to his father and remain a distant observer? Maybe he should pursue this enemy for his crimes? His heart said to bring him to justice. Quaid removed his hat and ran his fingers through his blonde wavy hair. Quaid was not accustomed to disobeying his father. He pondered how to reconcile all the revelations about his father's life. Lost in thought, Quaid looked up onto the desktop. There staring back at him was the Holy Bible. It was open. Quaid leaned forward to glance at the page. Quaid's vision locked on to Psalm 51. It had been underlined. Quaid's curiosity grew. He began to read. 'Have mercy on me O God, according to thy loving kindness, according unto the multitude of thy tender mercies blot out my transgressions. Wash me thoroughly from mine iniquity, and cleanse me from my sin. For I acknowledge my transgressions. And my sin is ever before me. Against thee, thee only, have I sinned, and done this evil in thy sight, that thou mightest be justified when thou speakest, and be clear when thou judgest. Behold, I was shapen in iniquity, and in sin did my mother conceive me. Behold, thou desirest truth in the inward parts, and in the hidden part thou shalt make me to know wisdom. Purge me with hyssop, and I shall be clean. Wash me, and I shall be whiter than snow. Make me to hear joy and gladness, that the bones which thou hast broken may rejoice. Hide thy face from my sins, and blot out all mine iniquities. Create in me a clean heart, O God, and renew a right spirit within me. Cast me not away from thy presence, and take not thy holy spirit from me. Restore unto me the joy of thy salvation, and uphold me with thy free spirit. Then will I teach transgressors thy ways, and sinners shall be converted unto thee. Deliver me from bloodguiltiness, O God, thou God of my salvation.'[31]

Quaid sat back in his chair. The words of the page spoke loudly in his ears. Quaid understood what his father was relaying to him. He relented on his repugnance. Revulsion renounced, Quaid reluctantly relocated his reflection to reality. His loving forgiveness for his father was vast, more, than he had realized. Quaid's love would not change.

Now, he had to act. What action to take, and what result would occur, he did not yet know. Quaid tried to clear his head. He rose and proceeded to the door. A ride on the open range would go a long way to put the last few days into perspective. Quaid climbed upon Angel, turned her around, and strode off.

Quaid's mind drifted with the wind that blew by him. He felt the power of Angel through his legs as he rode astride her back. The sun warmed his face. He took in all the beauty of nature. The landscape rolled in his eyes. The hills, the trees, the grass, the flowers, drew splendor from his soul. Quaid's mood improved as he traveled on. What wonders had God made. No artist could have painted it more vividly. No sculptor could have molded a more statuesque work. No poet could have penned a more dream-like composition as this.

Quaid strode on, in no particular direction. He just enjoyed the change in the frame of mind. Quaid thought of his youth. He thought of the pleasure of the days spent working with the animals on the farm. He thought of the good times with his companion Poe. Quaid thought of the hours they went exploring.

---

31   Holy Bible - Psalms 51

Through that exploration, Quaid found himself. Quaid recalled the past fondly. While reminiscing, Quaid recalled his friend's current condition. Quaid prayed silently for Poe's complete recovery. "Poe, 'Grace be with you, mercy, and peace, from God the father. And from the Lord Jesus Christ, the son of the father, in truth and love.'"[32] Afterward, Quaid thought of John Henry and little Samantha. It brought him back to earth. Quaid should check on their status, he thought. Without missing a stride, Quaid directed Angel to the colonel's old place.

As the day grew long, Quaid approached the house of the colonel. Quaid shouted as he rode up. He wanted John Henry to know that someone was approaching. He wanted him to know it was someone friendly. "John Henry! It is Marshall Quaid! Are you around?" Quaid announced.

Shortly thereafter, a large figure appeared at the door. It was John Henry. Quaid rode in closer. "Are you well, John?" asked Quaid.

"We are as good as can be expected," replied John Henry. "Would you like to come in for a spell?" he asked Quaid.

"Certainly, I could use a round of conversation," said Quaid.

Quaid dismounted. He climbed up the short steps to the porch, then, followed John Henry into the old wooden structure. Quaid walked behind John Henry down the straight and narrow hallway. Pictures of the colonel and his family lined the walls. Quaid's countenance became altered. He felt sad for Samantha's circumstance. Quaid walked on. John Henry finally stopped in the large open kitchen, the place where Quaid had found the

---

32   Holy Bible - II John 1:3

lifeless bodies of the colonel and his wife. John Henry pulled back a seat at the table, and addressed Quaid. "Would you like to sit, Marshall?"

"Yes, thank you," said Quaid.

"I hope you don't mind that we reside here. I am not too comfortable in the other rooms," said John Henry.

"Understandable," said Quaid. Quaid sat, "How's your health?" Quaid started up. He knew it was just small talk, but Quaid felt that he had to begin somewhere.

"I am well," replied John Henry.

"And Samantha, is she well?" asked Quaid.

"As well as one who has lost her parents can be, Marshall," said John Henry.

"I am truly sorry, John," said Quaid.

"Please, do not trouble yourself so," said John Henry. "You did more than most by rescuing me and Sam. We are in your debt."

"I did the easy work, John," said Quaid. "The truly difficult times lay ahead. You will have hard days raising a child. So, if you need anything John, let me know."

"Thank you, for your offer Marshall. We will be fine. I love Sam like my own life. I will see that she knows that. There is nothing greater than a father's love for his child," said John Henry.

Quaid became quiet all of a sudden. Quaid's loss of words struck John Henry hard. John Henry felt Quaid's trepidation for the situation.

"May I tell you something?" asked John Henry.

"Why yes," said Quaid.

"Let me ask you Marshall, do you know of II Timothy?" asked John Henry. Quaid was silent, still. John Henry continued. "'At my first answer no man stood with me, but all men forsook me. I pray God that it may not be laid to their charge. Notwithstanding the Lord stood with me, and strengthened me, that by me the preaching might be fully known, and that all the Gentiles might hear. And I was delivered out of the mouth of the lion. And the Lord shall deliver me from every evil work, and will preserve me unto his heavenly kingdom.'"[33]

Quaid was visibly moved.

John Henry continued. "You see, Marshall, your father stood with me when all others did not. I can only express thankfulness to God for him. I cried out to heaven. God sent your father. He displayed great valor. It is not easy to do what God wants, and not what man wants. He saved my life, Marshall, and many others. Do not condemn him quickly. Marshall, rest easy in the knowledge, that liberty and justice were served."

Quaid was quiet and contemplative. After a time, Quaid spoke. "Thank you for those words, John. I needed to hear them."

John Henry stood up and walked past Quaid. "Now that history has been balanced, I say we eat," said John Henry.

Quaid, not having taken any nourishment all day, concurred. "I am hungry," said Quaid. "I could go for a morsel or two, if it is not too much trouble."

"Trouble?" questioned John Henry. "I enjoy preparing meals. First, however, I must call for my little helper." John Henry shouted. "Samantha!" After a short time, she appeared.

---

33   Holy Bible - II Timothy 4:16

"Hello Sam," said Quaid.

"Good evening Marshall," Samantha answered.

Without a further word, they all pitched in to make dinner. It began to get dark, as they all sat down to eat. John Henry turned his gaze toward Samantha. "Can you say grace?" John Henry asked.

Samantha nodded. With little hesitation, Samantha, in her diminutive, angelic voice began, "Bless us, O Lord, and these your gifts, which we are about to receive from your bounty, through Christ our Lord. Amen." As the day turned to night, the despair in Quaid's heart turned to light.

At the end of the evening, Quaid had one more stop to make. He wanted to check in on an old friend. As Quaid mounted Angel in the dark light of the moon, he thought, maybe no news was good news. His life without his father had been difficult, however, his best friend had always been at his side. Riding Angel towards town, Quaid recalled how Poe would run out in front as he rode. "Poe protect!" came the call. As the words rolled out over his lips, Poe would advance his position in double time to complete the reconnaissance. At any sign of man or beast, a loud howl would split the air, giving warning to young Quaid. His presence was comforting, calming. Now without him in front, Quaid felt a torrid wave of agitation.

Quaid reached the town's main road. He quickly made for the doctor's office with haste. Quaid wanted to arrive before the doc had retired for the evening. Quaid pulled up on Angel and dismounted. He strode up the stair, and rapped gently on the door. It was soft, but rapid enough to relay his need to enter. A light from inside was seen. It slowly increased in intensity. The door came ajar. There stood the doctor still wearing his daytime attire.

"Come to see your friend, Marshall?" asked the doctor.

"Yes, if it is not too inconvenient," said Quaid.

"Nonsense," said the doctor.

"Come right in," he said.

Quaid quickly moved forward but had some apprehension in his heart. It skipped a beat. His arrhythmia led to tachycardia, as Quaid looked around the room for Poe.

"He is doing well," said the doctor. He continued. "He is responding to treatment. He also took in some food today. The best sign is that I believe he snarled a little at me. I guess that old spunk is coming back."

Quaid saw a large cage in the corner. In it a large fur-filled husk lay on its side. Quaid walked over to him.

"Poe," said Quaid quietly. With that, the slumbering wolf awoke. Poe tilted his head to see a smiling Quaid. Quaid knelt down close to Poe's ear. He whispered, "Poe, I am here." Poe's mouth moved but no sound was made. "Stay still buddy, do not get up," said Quaid. "Conserve your strength."

Quaid stood. He walked over to the doctor.

"How is he really doing Doc?" Quaid asked.

"He has good vital signs. There is no evidence of infection. He is eating now, and producing good urine," said the doctor.

"How much longer will it be before he recovers?" asked Quaid.

"It is difficult to tell with animals, Marshall. I usually deal in human terms," said the doctor.

"I understand," said Quaid "Take good care of him, doc. He is all I have."

"Your friend is getting the best care available," said the doctor. "I am confident he will be at your side again soon."

With that, Quaid tipped his hat. He did not want to seem too emotional, but inside his heart was heavy. The news was good, and for that, Quaid was thankful. Quaid strode out into the darkness once again. He began to take that long, lonely ride home.

CHAPTER 10

Booth and the boys huddled near the warm campfire. All were full of food and not very talkative. The woods, broad brush, and rock, encircled them. The vegetation gave more than adequate cover. Tall trees darted up, covering the countryside. The towering trunks of wood rose like spikes, creating a cascading cage of impenetrable projections. They extended high into the night sky, with a thickly carved bark, and branches which appeared to be reaching for the stars. Clouds hung in the atmosphere blocking out the moon. Darkness shone. With the exception of the glow from the fire, the plane was devoid of light. Booth, being the keen strategist, had himself positioned for a quick escape. Having been chased for years; looking over one's shoulder, does that to a man. This evening, however, Booth seemed relaxed in this woodland retreat. The eclipsed moon and impotent wind had the botanicals making little sound. Other than the occasional chirp from the nocturnal inhabitants, all was still. Booth's accomplices were scattered in various locations. Most were in close proximity to the radiating flames of the fire. Some were sitting on blankets. Others reclined against the formation of rock. It created a pit-like palace for these vipers.

Booth suddenly stood, and began to speak. "Well boys, tomorrow it will all be over. Yet, it will also begin." The ragged band of bandits seemed to acknowledge in the affirmative, as each sipped on his chickaree. Booth's voice seemed to boom out over the camp as if he had been shouting from a mountain top. "This time, the choirboy will not be able to save himself. Isolated and alone, we will take him. And like all men, he will become tired and hungry. We will break him like bread, my brethren!" Booth began to pace back and forth as a caged cat. He continued his rant. "He will be beaten. Then, when bludgeoned and bloodied, he will crack and cry out for a rescue. With death approaching, the temptation of a life of riches in our new world will see him on his knees. Once we have him, we have Black."

Booth stopped. All was quiet. Booth's senses became more attentive. His exterior seemed to change like a chameleon crawling across greens. With a pompous pride, Booth went on. Now, however, a new slant had struck his tone. "'Remember March! Did not the great Julius bleed for justice sake? What villain touched his body that did stab. And, not for justice? What, shall one of us, that struck the foremost man of all this world, but for supporting robbers, shall we now!'" [34]

The men were perplexed. They had seen these signs of slipping sanity before. Booth orated now with even more

---

34   William Shakespeare - Julius Caesar Act IV Scene 3

punctuation. This was real to him. Shakespeare's masterpiece, the Roman saga, was as vivid as his own hand in front of his face. The men looked around at each other. Was this, the actor, playing a part; or the part playing an actor? As the men gazed at their embattled leader, one of the grey-coats spoke out. "When do we attack?"

Booth's eyes exploded, nostrils flared, and his agitation increased. "'I'll know his humor when he knows his time. What should the wars do with these jiggling fools?'"[35]

The bandits sat still, seemingly stunned. The question had been asked and answered. Yet to the men in grey the plan had not been clarified. Another conspirator raised his voice to question his commander. "Shall we attack, or wait until the enemy seeks us?"

Booth leapt back into his narrative. "'Do stand but in a forced affection, for they have grudged us contribution. The enemy marching along by them, by them shall make a fuller number up. Come on refreshed, new added, and encouraged, from which advantage shall we cut him off. If at Philippi we do face him there, the people at our back.'"[36]

No sooner had the words passed across Booth's lips, he appeared startled. He was not struck by sound, but by a smell. It was a pungent smell. It was a familiar smell. It was one he had not perceived in some time. The fumes flowed out of the brush, and danced around the fire like a bean. "Yes. Yes! That's it!" cried Booth. Beans, coffee beans; the smell of coffee had hit Booth's nostrils like a tidal wave. As it all washed across Booth's brain, mechanics were set in motion. Booth cried, "Move!"

---

35   William Shakespeare - Julius Caesar Act IV Scene 3

36   William Shakespeare - Julius Caesar Act IV Scene 3

A quick burst sent a change streaming through the air. A loud thud struck. One of the grey-coated criminals slumped over, dead. Looking down, the others could see a large knife protruding from his neck. A flood of blood poured over him like the Red Sea receding over Pharaoh. "Move!" Booth exclaimed again.

No longer willing to wait, Booth turned and raced into the darkness. As the others struggled to grab their weapons, saddles, and possessions, another change in the wind came. Woosh! A hawk-like dart pierced the chest of another grey coat. Heart still pumping, it pushed the life fluid out in spurts. The body fell like lumber, leaving a scattered spray of ruby in the dirt. The corpse hit flat. The impact spewed dust out in a cloud around the carcass.

The two opposite the dead, leapt to their horses. A single hitch started the equine exit. The massive musculature marauded into the thick. Pounding harried hoofs, struck the sediment. Repetitive strikes pulsated up into the air like drums throbbing violently. As the grey-coats weaved through the woods, a barrage of projectiles appeared, baring their escape. The arrows pierced the night air in rapid succession. Streaming stems of steel exploded into the dermis. The sharp quills struck the fleeing foes legs, shoulders, and backs. They ripped the flesh like a raptor. Each arrow dug in, drew blood, and produced pain. The metal tips cut through the cutis, propelling the pursued off their transports. The grey-coats dropped off each ride like stones falling from the sky.

Booth scrambled away from the point of attack at top speed. He weaved in and out of the tall trees as fast as his legs could carry him without stumbling. Booth ran in no apparent direction. The cries of his fallen conspirators could be heard echoing from behind. His pulse had quickened, and his breathing became labored. The thick undergrowth slapped at Booth's thighs as he sped forward. His hurried retreat had not gone unnoticed. A bold black figure came hurling out of the thicket. Barely discernable in the dark, it moved with a powerful push. It churned like a locomotive, as steam puffed forth from the front. The combustive coal-like eyes fuelled its fury forward. The inferno drove through the brush, thrusting it aside as dust in the wind. Behind the moving mauler, the soil flung out like a comets' tail. Multiple missiles again filled the dark sky. The whistling rain poured out its precipitation, impaling a path of preclusion from escape. Booth evaded each ethereal arrow. He reached the bank of a deep flowing river. There a small craft was anchored, awaiting his arrival. Booth boarded, shoved off, and was immediately caught by the raging rapids. He disappeared behind the cloak of the current like a curtain dropping.

The last man standing at the camp was frozen in fear. A feeling of dread drained the color from his face. The wind, then, seemed to pick up. It spun him around like a twister. The force was felt as fingers tightening around his throat. The captive could hardly move any air with which to speak. The whirlwind raised him up. As the grey-coat's feet left the ground, he glanced down. There at the end of an enormous arm was Black.

"Yell now, Rebel," said Black.

No answer came.

"Not even a cry for help?" asked Black. He continued, "I suppose not, for there is no help for you, where are you going."

Black increased the pressure around the grey-coat's larynx.

"What is planned for my son?" asked Black.

The rebel coughed. The only thing that came forth from his mouth was blood-tinged saliva. Black shook him like a leaf. Still, there was no reply. The lack of response was of no consequence to Black. Thus, he crushed the trachea of the traitor with one motion. The limp carcass struck the ground like an empty sack.

Black turned. His ears pricked up. No horse hooves were heard. Black's face reflected his frustration. No information, and even worse; there was no Booth. A long nights work, all for naught, he thought. Black turned his attention to the campsite. He rummaged through each of the grey-coats scattered belongings looking for clues. Where was Booth going? Black thought. What was he planning next? With all the adrenaline Black could barely think. He threw blankets, pans, and packs around. Black overturned the saddle bags, and kicked over the tent stakes; nothing. On the opposite side of the campfire Black saw a small periodical. He leapt over to it like a leopard. Black picked up the manuscript. He brushed off the dust from the cover. The title read, 'Julius Caesar.' One page corner had been turned down. Black opened it and began to read.

"'All this! Aye, more. Fret til your proud heart break. Go show your slaves how choleric you are. And make your bondmen tremble. Must I budge? Must I observe you? Must I stand and crouch under your testy humour? By the gods, you shall digest the venom of the spleen, though it do split you; for from this day forth I'll use you for my mirth, yea, for my laughter, when you are waspish."[37]

Black closed the text. He straightened up and took a deep breath. There in the light of the fire, he was vulnerable. It was time to disappear. He did just that. Black faded into the dark from which he came, gone.

---

37   William Shakespeare - Julius Caesar Act IV Scene 3

Chapter 11

Daybreak found Quaid sitting on the edge of his bed, contemplating all that had transpired. His run in with Booth, meeting his father, the stampede; they all crossed his mind as he prepared for yet another day. How was he to make sense of it, he thought. And, once he did, how to proceed? Quaid pondered. Should he try to capture Booth? Should he go looking for his father? Should he alert the townspeople? Quaid wondered. It was like a game, a game of chess. All of the complicated moves clouded the conscious of the contemplative Quaid. Maybe, he thought, it was not chess. Maybe, it was more simplistic. Just maybe, it was checkers. Like checkers, all Quaid had to do was keep moving forward. Quaid was to be a shark. He would be the great predator that keeps moving on the advance or dies. That was his lot in life, to pursue, to pursue and overtake. Now, he just had to find a starting point.

Quaid was a man of faith. His whole life had been guided by God. Where else would Quaid turn when questions needed answers but to Him. Quaid realized that his first move was to go directly to God's house. He dressed. He saddled Angel. He rode to town. There, Quaid went directly to the chapel.

Quaid rode swiftly through town. There was no hesitation or delay to exchange pleasantries. Quaid arrived just outside the entry steps. He was in clear view of the escalating steeple. As Quaid glanced up, the sun shone down on him with the radiance of a diamond. On the top of the spire, the cross cast an image of comparative darkness over Quaid. The long shadow seemed to signify his sacrifice. Quaid was taken aback by the power of its pronouncement. Quaid continued to stare. It was more than a symbol to Quaid, it was life. He realized he was in the right place. Quaid looked down, his hat hid his features. Slowly, he ascended the staircase. Reaching the summit, Quaid grasped and pushed forth on the handle of the large wooden door of the church. It creaked as it moved. Quaid strode in, and politely sealed the portal.

As Quaid turned, he beheld the majesty of the altar. The reredos was hand-painted beauty. Above the savior hanging from the cross was a dove, descending from heaven. It had a coat of gold spreading far from its white wings to the very top of the structure. As Quaid glanced up from the alabaster bird, he felt the Holy Spirit fill him as it did the mural. The altar table was draped with a purple cloth, the color of kings. On it, the insignia of two intersecting lines was displayed. White columns rose up from the ground, creating an arched entrance. The contrasting dark wooden pews lined the processional path.

About halfway down the aisle, Quaid looked over to see the back of the priest darting into the confessional. Quaid stopped.

He turned, then with his long gait, proceeded across to the confessional entrance. Quaid opened the door, and sat down with a small thud.

There was silence. After a short while, the screen was pushed back forcefully. Quaid began rather softly. "Forgive me father, for I have sinned." No reply. Quaid cleared the frog from his throat. He continued, "I am troubled by an ethical dilemma." Quaid stopped and waited for a response. Finally, the priest said, "Go on."

"My father plans to kill a man," said Quaid. Again, nothing came from the other side. Quaid continued, "There is no doubt that this man has done evil. But father, I do not believe in murder."

"What do you believe?" asked the priest.

"I believe in justice," answered Quaid.

"How do you define justice?" asked the priest.

"Justice is defined by the law, "replied Quaid.

The priest responded, '"The law of the Lord is perfect, reviving the soul. The testimony of the Lord is sure, making wise the simple. The precepts of the Lord are right, rejoicing the heart. The commandment of the Lord is pure, enlightening the eyes.'"[38]

Quaid processed the words of the psalmist. His eyes had been opened. His heart at the ready, Quaid thought back to the days of his Bible lessons as a boy. He recalled the wisdom his father had passed down to him through those teachings. Quaid would follow the Lord's commandments. It seemed so clear.

---

38   Holy Bible - Psalms 19:7

Quaid had one more query. "Father, I will follow the law, but where am I to start," asked Quaid.

"' The effectual fervent prayers of a righteous man availeth much,'"[39] replied the priest.

"I see father," said Quaid. "I will pray."

There was a short silence.

"'Be careful for nothing, but in every thing; by prayer and supplication with thanksgiving let your requests be made known unto God,'"[40] said the priest with a firm tone.

Quaid knew that accent. He had heard it every Sunday, but not in church. It was in his youth at his father's knee. Quaid sat up straight and quick. He inquired, "Pappy?"

"Yes, Jacob," came the reply from the other side. Quaid's eyes widened. The voice continued, "It is I, your father," said Black.

"Why are you here?" asked Quaid.

"I merely come when I am called." said Black. There was a contemplative quiet, as Quaid rolled that response around in his head. Black then continued, "Need I remind you of what you already know to be true? Jacob, you are not just my son, but also God's." Again there was silence. Black proceeded. "Nothing can give me more pride than seeing that you place God's law above all else."

Quaid was struck by the sentiment. The flattery aside, Quaid fired back. "Then you will not pursue and kill Booth?"

"Kill, no. Pursue, yes," said Black.

"How do you plan to find him," asked Quaid.

---

39   Holy Bible - James 5:16
40   Holy Bible - Philippians 4:6

"Jacob, Booth is not just evil, he is insane. Recall your literature, son. In Shakespeare's portrayal, Marcus Brutus led his band out of the hills to the plains of Phillipi around the three o'clock hour. Phillipi will be the location where Brutus awaits Anthony and Octavious. Do you know of such a landscape that could mirror those haunts?"

Quaid stepped out of the confessional. Black quickly followed. Quaid glanced over at his father's face. It was as if the years melted away like a spring snow. Quaid was again, a young lad looking for his father's acceptance. Quaid could no longer keep himself wrapped in his own anger. Quaid realized that he loved his father, for better or for worse. Quaid now understood that Black's past actions were conceived in love, a love for him.

"Yes, I know of such a place," said Quaid.

"'Then cry havoc, and let slip the dogs of war. That this foul deed shall smell above the earth with carrion men, groaning for burial,'"[41] replied Black.

"What?" asked Quaid.

"Join me, on the attack," said Black. "Do you think only a thespian can quote Shakespeare?"

"Apparently, not," said Quaid with a small air of sarcasm. Quaid continued with a more profound tone, "It seems after all these years, I have still underestimated you, father."

"Let us hope that Booth has done the same," said Black.

---

41   William Shakespeare – Julius Caesar act III Scene 1

Chapter 12

Quaid and Black approached the plain under the late afternoon heat of the one western town's sun. The horses slowly approached the wooded edge of an open range, just out of the sight of any of the grey gang. As Black drew Demon near the plain's barrier of woods, he put up his hand and said, "Hold!" His position still concealed, Black dropped down from Demon to the ground. Black bent down on one knee as if praying. Black tipped back the brim of his hat, ever so slightly, to get a better look at the battlefield.

Just yards away from Black, was open ground. It was vast and flat. It had a few scattered rocks, mostly at the sides, extending north. Black surveyed the field closely. He realized the ground inclined slowly. At the opposite end of the plain there was a series of rock formations. This could provide excellent cover. Black's head dropped.

"What is it Pappy?" asked Quaid.

"I have seen battlefields like this before. Only this time, you and I are on the receiving end," said Black.

Quaid looked at his father, perplexed. Black, seeing his son did not grasp the significance of his findings continued, "Gettysburg, Gettysburg, my son. It is Pickett's charge in reverse. On a July day, a few years past, the Confederate army mounted a full assault on the Union position from across an inclined grassy knoll. The Union's artillery, combined with the advantage of the high ground lead to the annihilation of the southern force that day. That battle turned the tide of the war."

Quaid knelt down next to Black.

"What is the plan then?" Quaid asked.

"We must nullify their strength by exploiting their weakness," said Black.

"Go on," said Quaid, as he stared at his father with a savage intensity.

"We must use cover," said Black.

"Thus we will use the cloak of night. At dusk, I want you to make your way around to those rocks on Booth's left flank." Black extended his arm and pointed as he spoke. At daybreak you must start your guns blazing. Fire a rapid succession of suppressing rounds to allow for protection and distraction. I will circle around to the left and take up the position on the right flank." Black again signaled his intentions with his forefinger. "You will draw their fire."

"Then what?" asked Quaid.

"Then, we wait," said Black.

Quaid, looking concerned and confused, replied, "Wait for what? Death!" Quaid's words came out with a stern irony.

Black placed his large bear-like hand on Quaid's shoulder. "Do not fear. Booth will not know I am present, this is our advantage. Booth will assume he has you in check. His ego will take over. Once that happens, he will begin to move on you. You must be prepared to handle an array of attack configurations. Keep moving, keep low, and no matter what transpires, keep fighting. I will take care of the rest."

Quaid looked deep into his father's opulent eyes of green, stern and steadfast. His chin of stone, the chiseled nose, installed a confidence through strength. Quaid had no fear. Trust in his earthly father never wavered. Quaid nodded in the affirmative, then, nightfall.

Quaid loaded himself down with ammunition. He let the weight of the rounds engage gravity, and he dropped onto his abdomen. Quaid crawled, slow and low. Quaid was so low he could taste the dust in his mouth. The sand was still hot, and it felt warm against his exposed skin. Quaid crawled on through the darkness. As he skirted across the ground, Quaid's sweat dripped from his face. It left a remanent in the soil like a snake shedding his skin. Quaid drew closer. It was quiet. It was so quiet Quaid could hear his own heart beat. Determined, Quaid moved ever forward, deliberately. After what seemed like an eternal voyage, Quaid reached a small shelter of stone. It was only a hundred yards away from the end of the plain. Here justice would be delivered. Numbers were not in Quaid's favor, but the savvy gunslinger had gone against the odds before. He rested, and waited.

Daybreak came. Quaid pulled both six guns from his holster, rose up, and squeezed off round after round in the direction of the rock fortress at the end of the plain. At first there was no motion. No sight or sound of an enemy was to be found. Quaid stared into the silence. In a cloudburst, fire came raining down upon his position. Quaid dove for shelter as the bullets showered down around him. As it poured projectiles, Quaid hit the turf with a thud. Just behind a small peak of protection in the rock, Quaid was enveloped by the ballistic barrage. Almost without hesitation, Quaid sat up, spun and returned volley. Quaid could clearly see the bobbing heads of the advancing grey-coats. Flashes of gunfire reflected off the surrounding stone in an illuminous electric discharge. Quaid pulled back to reload. He took this opportunity to look at the wooded canopy behind him. There was no sign of father. Quaid guessed that he had already slipped away. It now appeared to Quaid that Black's plan had wings, but could the flight be sustained. That was still uncertain.

Quaid again let loose with more missiles. The sound echoed across the plain and returned as thunderous bolts. Quaid saw one, maybe two men fall back wounded. Quaid calmly laid low in the stronghold of the stone blockade. Bullets hailed, chipping pieces of calculi into the air. This was a fight, a fierce fight. Quaid wondered, was this just the first conflict of a battle, or the chiseled formation of his tombstone?

The firing stopped. Quaid listened intently but heard nothing. Again he reloaded. Quaid could not help but think the enemy was on the move. That is what he would do. Outflank the flanker; that would be the logical tact. Quaid reached out his neck and peered to his right. There the terrain became hilly, rocky, and spattered with brush. Quaid's vision scanned the contours of the canyon. A gentle breeze blew. Some of the small branches bent under it's warm breath. In the distance Quaid's eyes perceived more movement than just the wind's benevolent blow. The enemy was coming, and coming fast. Quaid decided not to engage them just yet. He waited. All invisible actions continued, as the enemy closed on Quaid. There was a quiet calm. Quaid took a breath, raised his voice and exclaimed, "Booth, do not run, or I will be forced to fire." Quaid needed to know his adversary's coordinates. Quaid awaited a reply. Any response could be used to triangulate positions. He hoped Booth would take the bait.

"Very good, choirboy, but our passion play has not yet ended."

"Your day is done," shouted Quaid.

"'For it is easier for heaven and earth to pass away, than for one dot of the law to become void.'"[42]

"Words on a page, choirboy!"

Again silence. Quaid repositioned himself. They would be coming soon. Quaid silently slid from the rock across the dirt into the dense thicket. He stopped and looked one hundred and eighty degrees, no enemy. Quaid began to think. How many were coming? From where? At what angle? Was another onslaught eminent? Quaid decided to keep moving, slithering quickly underbrush. A loud click pricked his ears. Quaid looked up from his position on the ground, to see three men in a scattered formation, approaching. The point man was holding a pistol directed at Quaid. He froze.

"Seems like our choirboy is more like a snake in the grass," said the lead.

---

42   Holy Bible - Luke 16:17

"There will be no victory for you," said Quaid.

"No?" questioned the lead. "It seems to me that you are at a disadvantage."

Quaid stood up. He looked to see the face of the man advancing toward him.

"Now then choirboy, toss your gun out." said the lead.

Surrounded, Quaid swung his arm forward to discard his weapon. While doing so, Quaid saw the face of his enemy. To Quaid's embarrassment, it was not Booth.

"You see, choirboy, not only have you been deceived, you have been had."

Quaid displayed an angry stare. Dejected, he dropped his head. Disgusted, yet unable to admit defeat, Quaid shook his head slightly. "'The folly of fools is deceit.'"[43] said Quaid. As he spoke those words, a growing growl came rising off the ground, and caught the winds of the plain. A large grey wolf sprang from the source of the sound, toppling the lead conspirator. In the commotion, Quaid quickly drew down. Pulling out his boot blade, Quaid flung it into the chest of a second conspirator with one smooth motion. The grey-coat grabbed at his chest, as if his beating heart was being pulled from its cage. Dropping down to his knees, the blood pumped out of the wound like a geyser, reddening the sand. Quaid jumped back like a grasshopper, crouching behind the protection of the rock. Bullets sprayed his position. Quaid waited patiently for an opening. The spitting spray stopped. Quaid sprang out and released his waist dagger. Through the ether it traveled. It lodged in the third bandit's shoulder setting off a blast from the grey-coat's gun.

---

43   Holy Bible - Proverbs 14:8

The explosion blew the dust from the ground. Being knocked backward by the blade, the conspirator regained his balance. Quaid had already advanced. Quaid reached back with all his might and let go with a punch that sent blood spewing from the grey-coat's mouth. Quaid followed up with a left uppercut that sent him supine. Reaching to retrieve his weapon, the fallen strained his outstretched arm. Simultaneously, the conspirator and Quaid grabbed the gun. Quaid wrapped his hands around the grey-coat's wrist as they wrangled for the weapon. Quaid firmly forced the cylinder to his chest and squeezed off two rounds. The life drained from the fallen's face. Quaid stood, towering above him like a gladiator.

Quaid looked over at Poe. He saw that Poe had the enemy well in hand, or in this case, teeth. Poe had placed his razor sharp incisors across the grey-coat's throat, immobilizing him. Quaid smiled. "It is good to see you back to form my old friend," he said. Quaid approached Poe's position. Looking down at the paralyzed opponent, Quaid questioned, "Where is Booth?" No answer came. Quaid grasped his shirt, and pulled firmly, flipping him face down. He bound him with rope, and sat him up. Once more with his hands clenched across his collar, Quaid queried in anger, "Where is John Wilkes Booth?"

On the other side of the plain, a man on a horse rode hard. It was away from Quaid's direction. As the shots rang out from Quaid's struggle with the conspirators, the horse held up. It spun around, facing the sound of the battle. The horseman was Booth. Booth was making his escape under the guile of pretense. A voice echoed out. It made Booth's head swivel.

"Running again, coward?" said the voice. "It seems the only way you will face a man is at his back."

Booth's eyes targeted the source. There, sitting atop Demon was Matthan Quaid. "Black!" Booth exclaimed with disgust. Unwilling to be beaten, Booth kicked his mount with all his strength. Whipping the reins, he fled. Black pursued. Demon bolted after him with a dark fury. The horse's hooves pounded the earth, as the two man stampede crushed the crust underneath. The dust blew back from the flight in a sandstorm. Booth pushed hard, moving forward over the nape of his horse's neck, throwing all is weight into the escape. Black followed in kind. Demon was powerful in motion. The Morgan pulled Black through the torrent. On the back side of the tornado, Black drew his bow with full force. He released the projectile with precision. It pierced through the pursuit, driving deep into the galloping quadriceps of Booth's ride. Black followed with fury, releasing an entire armament of arrows. Each struck hard. Coin, croup, dock, and stifle were struck. The penetrating wedges brought down the retreating rebel. As his steed slammed into the ground, Booth was ejected, landing in a heap. Booth turned to view his pursuer. Black closed in on Booth fast. Booth quickly got up, and ran. Black let loose, like lightening, a long blade. The time traveling toothpick plunged into Booth's thigh. Booth grabbed at the pain. He fell forward, striking the ground. Booth crumbled in a cloud of dust. Black leapt off Demon and approached on foot. The predator had his prey in sight. Time slowed as Booth struggled to his feet, his pant leg soaked in red. Once up, Booth staggered toward a rocky ravine just behind him. Booth looked for some kind of refuge but the cage was closing. Again the air split. A small dagger broke the tattered clothing at Booth's left arm. Blood poured from the wound. The agony seared through him. Booth teetered to one side, then, dropped to one knee in an effort to stabilize himself. Booth reacted by reaching for his sidearm. Another spike landed dead center, right shoulder. Booth clutched for the knife and cried out, "'I shall have glory by losing this day more than Octavious or Marc Anthony. By this vile conquest shall attain unto.'"[44]

Booth impacted and impaled, hit the ground prone. Black continued forward. Standing above, Black towered over the fallen form which was John Wilkes Booth. Now, the man was merely a huddled mass of flesh in a sanguineous pool. Black peered down searching for signs of life. With the toe of his large size twelve boot, Black rolled Booth supine. No respiration. No reflex. After what seemed like an age, Booth's mouth moved. He spoke softly, "'Night hangs upon my eyes, my bones would rest. That have but labored to attain this hour.'"[45]

Black responded, "If you are expecting a gentlemen's respect, you are quite mistaken. Black began to circle him. "However, I do not plan to end your life in this desolate sand. Your death will be better savored by the crowds at the Union gallows."

As Booth lay lifeless, it was difficult to ascertain whether or not he could comprehend Black's words. Maybe he was just not willing to comply. Black continued his dissertation. "If I must, I will carry you all the way to Washington." Still, there was no motion. No attempt to stand. Black bent down to gather his game. He reached over Booth's body to pull him up over his

---

44   William Shakespeare - Julius Caesar Act V Scene 5

45   William Shakespeare - Julius Caesar Act V Scene 5

shoulder. With one arm, up he went. Now, with Black occupied by his burden, Booth whispered, "How did you find me?"

Black relied, "I followed your lead."

"Lead?" questioned Booth.

"Yes," said Black. "In the final battle, Brutus attempted to escape by exiting on the opposite side of the battlefield."

Booth remained silent.

"Wonderfully written, wouldn't you say?" said Black.

As Black carried Booth on his shoulder like a sack of flour, a revolution of new life revived in the inanimate enemy. A once dormant Booth reached down and drew back Black's Bowie from him. Sensing a motion to strike, Black pushed Booth back off his perch, with force. Booth landed like a cat. Black's hand readied his revolver with a speed unseen. Black perceived his nemesis would flee but instead, he hesitated.

"'Farewell Caesar, now be still.'"[46] babbled Booth. In a blink of an eye, Booth ran himself through on the short sword, ending his life. Booth's body bobbled; then in a blink, he blindly blew over, belly up.

Quaid came running forth. Seeing Booth dead, he turned toward his father. Quaid could see that Black had not struck the final blow. Quaid let loose with a small smile. He was pleased to see his father still standing. As Quaid approached Black, he could see his emerald eyes glistening. The satisfaction of seeing his son reflected in the enlarging orbs, under a setting sun. Black holstered his weapon. "'So call the field to rest, and lets away,'"[47] said Black.

---

46   William Shakespeare - Julius Caesar Act V Scene 5
47   William Shakespeare - Julius Caesar Act V Scene 5

Quaid understood fully. The play had concluded. Justice was done. Black placed his arm around Quaid's shoulder. Father and son turned and walked slowly from the scene. As they walked, Quaid said softly, "Yes, too many ghosts."

Outside Quaid's ranch, the Marshall walked over to Demon. Black sat on his back and looked down at his son. John Henry and Samantha were present for the send off. Black, never much for words, did not address his son presently. Quaid peered up at Black and said, "Where will you go, Pappy?"

Black pulled on Demon's reins and spun him around. He stopped and looked back at Quaid. "I go where God calls me." said Black.

Quaid, realizing his time with his father was now very short, asked, "Will I see you again?"

"God willing," replied Black. "God willing."

Just before Black could kick start his ride; John Henry, moved by the moment, began singing. John Henry engaged his tremendous tenor voice. He started with a resounding, 'My eyes have seen the glory of the coming of the Lord...'

Black turned and trotted off, as the Battle Hymn of the Republic echoed in their ears.

End.

Made in the USA
Las Vegas, NV
28 February 2023

68303562R00083